INTO HOT WATER

A FOUR CORNERS MYSTERY

Judith Ann Isaacs

Butterfly & Bear Press
Jemez Pueblo, NM

Into Hot Water

A Four Corners Mystery

Judith Ann Isaacs

Copyright ©2014
ISBN 978-0-962964-58-9

Butterfly & Bear Press
95 Vista Hermosa Rd.
Jemez Pueblo, NM 87024
www.butterflyandbearpress.com

Cover and book design by Erica Kane; cover photo by the author.
Manufactured in the United States of America.

Other books by this author:

Guide to the Jemez Mountain Trail, Butterfly & Bear Press, Second edition, 2009

Jemez Valley Cookbook: The Food, The Land, The People, Butterfly & Bear Press, Second edition, 2006

Coming in 2016, the second Four Corners mystery: *River of Time*, also from Butterfly & Bear Press

To my children,
Elizabeth and Gregory,
authors both

ACKNOWLEDGMENTS

This book was many years in the making. Over that time, I received invaluable advice and support from my late husband, John R. Cook; he is always in my heart. Also, I met with writer's groups in New Mexico and Washington State. Thanks to Janine and Marc Brodine and Barbara Ranger-Lynch, my first readers; Erica Kane and Linda Sweet, discerning critics and relentless cheerleaders; and Michelle Miller Allen and Elizabeth McBride, both of whom were an inspiration as writers and as strong women.

jai 2014

CHAPTER 1

Amelie Jameson never tired of looking at the red sandstone cliffs, amazed at how the colors changed hour by hour. Right now, the harsh mid-day sun had wiped out the deepest hues, but even so she thought this was the most beautiful place in New Mexico. Leaning on the porch railing of the Cañon Springs marshal's office, she looked over the plaza and down the two-lane highway, which followed the meandering curves of the Jemez River.

The Cañon de San Diego narrowed at this point, funneling hundreds of cars through the Village of Cañon Springs and into the speed trap laid by the marshal and his deputies. Out-of-town visitors—and there were many on this Fourth of July—couldn't believe a state highway had been completely closed for the parade. The resulting backup had raised both temperatures and tempers inside the cars, trucks and RVs that sat bumper-to-bumper on the burning asphalt.

For as far as she could see in either direction, vehicles were parked haphazardly in the weeds at the highway's edge. Visitors in patriotic-themed tee shirts and various sun-blocking hats headed toward the teeming plaza. Many would stay until the last skyrocket had been fired from the American Legion fireworks display tonight, said by local civic boosters to be exceptionally glorious for a small town. Cañon Springs, with a population of less than 400, nestled beside the Jemez River, a handful of ancient adobe buildings under even more ancient cottonwoods. Beyond the river, piñon and juniper greened the slopes, and then gave way to sheer red sandstone that met mesa tops 1,500 feet above on both sides.

She had opted to wear a plain red tank top with navy blue shorts – a nod to Independence Day colors. Hiding her short brown curls was a wide-brimmed straw hat with a leather band studded with silver and turquoise—one of her favorite things to wear—a gift from her best friend, Lena Harris. While Amelie loved the small-town holiday celebration, she had not planned to be here today. An urgent email, really a SOS, from Lena had brought her over the Jemez Mountains from her home in Los Alamos. So much for a relaxed day off from her hectic work schedule—with no driving. But here she was, thankful she had managed to squeeze her Subaru into a spot near the plaza just before the highway was closed for the parade and glad to get this privileged viewing spot.

Marshal Carlton Duran stood at the other end of the porch on the old adobe that housed the marshal's office and municipal court. While otherwise in full uniform, he wore his lucky "Baca Ranch" cap pulled low over his eyes. His friends joked that he probably slept in the hat, but Amelie had reason to know that wasn't true. Even from this distance and separated by a dozen friends and acquaintances, she could tell he was still angry. Tension rose off him like heat waves off the highway. Since their last date a week ago, he had refused to speak to her, much less look at her. That's supposed to be a woman's trick, Amelie thought.

She made her way through the onlookers and touched Carlton's arm, evoking no response. "I'm going to the Bath House for a soak and massage in half an hour. Want to meet somewhere after the fireworks?" Still no response. She sighed. Okay, if that's the way he wanted to play it. Shaking her head, she stepped out of the shade and toward the growing mayhem in the plaza.

She hadn't come to see him anyway. She was here in response to Lena's plea for help, a last-minute trip from her home 35 miles away, because her friend had sounded—what? Desperate? Frightened? Ironically, they hadn't had a chance to talk yet. The Krazy Kokopelli B&B, owned by Lena and her husband, Walter, was full of holiday guests. Amelie knew that Lena had been moving at top speed since dawn, tending to her visitors. In fact, last time Amelie looked around, she hadn't even made it to the parade.

The parade had ended at the plaza with a final blast of sirens from the emergency vehicles, which were at least half the entries. The Hummingbird Music Camp band dissolved in front of the gazebo, kids dropping instrument cases in a pile and scattering to the booths that formed a circle at the plaza's edge. The Sheriff's Posse, still mounted on horseback, stepped carefully among them. Lining the parking area were homemade floats, including Smokey the Bear (Forest Service), a papier-mâché bookworm (library), and a plywood outhouse decorated with crepe paper (wastewater treatment plant). The smoky smell of barbeque mingled with the unique aroma of popcorn, all overlaid by the odor of dust rising from hundreds of shuffling feet.

Amelie stopped in the welcome shade of a canvas-covered booth. "Beautiful necklace," she said to a stunning blonde woman who was holding a delicate silver chain from which dangled a large crystal. The woman turned, and Amelie felt bathed by the light from her eyes. She had heard of violet eyes but had never before seen them on a real person.

The woman lifted the heavy weight of curly hair off her neck. She looked around with delight at the maelstrom of color and sound. Her jewelry reflected light from ears, throat, wrists, and ankles. Thin gold and silver chains of different lengths dropped into her cleavage, which partially obscured the charms and medallions that dangled from each strand. Rings gleamed from every finger and several toes, and bracelets set with a variety of stones adorned each arm. She was framed by crystals, amethysts and other semi-precious stones of many sizes dangling from the booth frame, sending slivers of rainbows in all directions. Everything about her sparkled.

She turned her gorgeous eyes back to Amelie and held out a hand. "Hi, I'm Maria," she said. "Don't you just love this place?" Dropping Amelie's hand, she twirled around, the necklace swinging in an arc that barely missed Amelie's face.

"Yes, I do," Amelie said, stepping back, ready to move on.

Maria continued, as though they were old friends, now holding the crystal in both hands. "I feel the energy coming from this one. Actually, I feel it surrounding this booth. Here, can't you feel it?" She held it out, still cupped in her two hands.

Amelie's inner debate on how much she wanted to engage this woman was interrupted by the man behind the counter. He looked up from his work of creating a similar necklace. "There's a mirror there if you want to try it on."

Maria continued her monologue, now directed to the audience of two. "I used to sleep with crystals all along the top of the headboard. Helped me to get clear about my path, showed me the light. That was how I knew it was time to come back. I grew up here, then lost my way, but now I know this is where I must be."

She again held the necklace between her and the sun, squinting as she tilted her head back. The mass of bright hair fell to the waist of her blue velvet broomstick skirt. "I used to make jewelry, but now I'm into herbs. Herbs and writing, writing poetry. Writing about life, about love, about all of this." Blonde hair flying, she whirled and flung out her arm again, nearly smacking an old lady who had wandered over to peer near-sightedly at the display.

Amelie smiled again, secretly amused at what she and Lena called "woo-woo" beliefs, not uncommon in the valley. Many people came here because they felt—or professed to feel—special, spiritual qualities in the land. She looked at the jewelry maker, who rolled his eyes. She made a moue in return, but in truth she often felt an almost indescribable aura around her here. She thought of herself as a practical, no-nonsense person, but she couldn't deny that this valley was different. Not today, crushed on all sides by the milling crowd, but in solitude, alone on a mesa top or a forest trail, she felt most at peace with herself and her world.

Maria's eyes rose to the mesa rising behind the village. She replaced the necklace and gave the man a sweet, loving smile. Her violet eyes glowed. "I feel the connection between us. I feel the connection to this place. To the healing waters." He nodded silently and went back to his work.

The starry-eyed blonde gazed at him benevolently, then turned back to Amelie. "This is almost like the necklace I lost last week," she said. "I think I'll come back and get it after my bath. I have an appointment soon." Raising her arms, she breathed deeply, then turned and floated in the direction of the Rio Jemez Bath House.

Amelie said a bland "good bye" to her back. She looked around again for Lena and sighted Walter, talking with another man, both sipping from aluminum to-go coffee cups. She made her way through the crowd and reached them in time to hear the man say, "I like your new show, man. Very cool. Very nice. I don't know how you do what you do with glass; yours is the best I've seen—and I've seen some fine glass sculpture in Seattle."

"Hi, Walter," she said. Lena's husband never liked to be called Walt.

"Hi, Amelie! This is my friend, Sage Hansen." Walter puffed on the pipe that seemed perpetually in his hand. "Sage and I have shown in a lot of the same galleries, and he has another show in Santa Fe this month."

She shook hands with the man, noting the bulging biceps and thick neck that said bodybuilder. Unlike Walter, in his khaki shorts and faded tee-shirt with a hole in one sleeve, Sage was spotlessly dressed in a light green polo shirt and jeans she would swear had been pressed. His blonde hair was cropped to nearly military precision. After a brief surveillance that scanned her body from head to toe, his eyes lingered on her cleavage where one wing of a butterfly tattoo peeked from her neckline. "Hi, Emily," he said.

"Hi, and not Emily. It's Amelie," she said, emphasizing the first syllable. She was accustomed to supplying the correct French pronunciation.

But Sage had resumed the conversation with Walter. "Yeah, and Santa Fe is the big time, man. But I've been all over since I saw you last. Besides Phoenix and Dallas, I've been to lots of little galleries in Utah and Arizona. I love being in this part of the country—for a visit, that is."

Walter tapped out his pipe on the sole of his Birkenstock sandal. "I still don't see why you live in Seattle when most of your shows are in the Four Corners."

"Too damn hot for me down here—like today." Despite his words, Sage looked cool, as though nothing in the environment touched him. "But everyone here likes my stuff, my Santa Fe colors, which I was doing before anyone called them that." He pushed a stone around with the toe of a leather shoe that had somehow managed to repel the dust. "What do you know about that new gallery . . ."

He broke off suddenly as though he'd spotted an art critic on the dusty road around the plaza. "My God. See that woman there —long blonde hair, blue velvet skirt. That's my girlfriend from Seattle. That's Maria. I cannot believe this." The cool demeanor vanished. His fists clenched until the knuckles were white. "She lied to me. She told me she was going to *Old* Mexico." He poured the dregs of his coffee onto the ground and without another word started toward the Bath House on a tangent that would intersect the woman's path.

Amelie raised her eyebrows, but Walter appeared not to find this behavior worthy of comment. "I just talked to that woman he's so upset with," she said. "Do you know her?"

"No, but Sage has girlfriends in a lot of places. He likes women."

She snorted. "I got that. Hey, I've been looking for Lena. Have you seen her?"

"No. We were swamped this morning, and I escaped and left her to clean up after breakfast." He sounded totally unrepentant. They chatted a few more minutes about the B&B, and then she started for the Bath House, once again pushing gently through the throng, reflecting on her many visits to Cañon Springs.

Hot springs were the reason the village existed. Mineral water bubbled from the ground along the river at temperatures ranging up to 190 degrees. The ancestral Jemez Pueblo people had settled here in the 1300s and called it —as closely as their language could be translated —place of hot water. For more than a century, visitors from Albuquerque and Santa Fe, afflicted with arthritis, rheumatism and other ailments, had been coming here to soak in the healing mineral baths. Today, at the turn of the 21st century, people still came to the historic whitewashed adobe Bath House, and Amelie never missed a chance for a soak when she came to town.

Getting a contract here had seemed like the greatest good luck at first. Lena was offering her a free room, and they would have time for walks and conversation. Amelie's one-woman consulting business, based in nearby Los Alamos, provided services to small towns throughout the Four Corners region of the Southwest. She loved the job she had created for herself, which was advising small town law enforcement and municipal courts on automation software and training employees to use the programs. The work involved constant travel, but she got to visit many places in the Four Corners where she wanted to go anyway to hike, camp, and soak in hot springs.

But once again, her predilection to get into sticky relationships had tripped her up. She had let herself have a fling with the Cañon Springs marshal, although a strong inner voice had said that would be a mistake— because he was a client and because they were very different personality types. Now, she regretted not listening to that voice.

Amelie passed booths of candles, herbal remedies, pottery, and more jewelry, oblivious to the crowd, mentally preparing herself to get through the next few weeks. The contract she had with the village stipulated that the marshal's office receive eight training sessions, and they had completed only three. She and Carlton would have to see each other several times in the next few months. Amelie resolved to let go of her frustration. Maybe something will happen to distract him. Maybe someone will cheat at the freckle-counting contest. The thought cheered her considerably, and she once again tuned into the holiday spirit, humming along as the music camp faculty, now installed in the gazebo, played "Stars and Stripes Forever."

Because she came to the Bath House every time she visited Cañon Springs, Amelie knew several of the attendants by name. This time it was a petite woman dressed in black named Serafina who led her through a small anteroom and into the woman's side of the building. Along one wall were four huge concrete tubs, separated by wooden partitions. Pipes three inches in diameter emerged from the wall over each tub, boldly labeled "Hot" and "Cold." Curtains completed the enclosures, giving each customer privacy in her tub. Along the other wall, women relaxing in an herbal wrap made mummy-like mounds on three high tables. Although Amelie had decided against a wrap today, she was frequently one of those bundled forms, sweating every last toxin out of her body.

Thanking Serafina, she pulled her curtain closed, stripped off her shorts, tee shirt and underwear and sank into the tub, adding more hot water until only her head was above water level. If a person who was 5'9" and wore a size 12 could be called a nymph, she was one. A water nymph. Soaking in hot water was almost as good as sex. She heard Serafina say, "Here's some more water, Maria." From this, she deduced that the blonde woman she had just met in the plaza was in the adjacent tub.

Eyes closed, she tried to put aside thoughts of Carlton, of her work, of Lena's mysterious and urgent problem. Murmuring voices and the soothing sound of an Indian flute from an overhead speaker faded into white noise in the background. Focusing on her breathing, she drifted into a dream state, unaware that outside the thick adobe walls strong emotions were building in more than one person, focused on the blonde woman in the next tub.

═══ CHAPTER 2 ═══

Across the street from the Bath House and unknown to each other, two dissimilar women had watched Maria move around the plaza. That she was oblivious to their presence made both of them angry, but for very different reasons.

Jenny Saunders sat on the deck of the Jemez River Bar and Grill, which she had learned was known simply as "the bar" to locals. After all, it was the only one for miles around. Her worn cowboy boots were propped on the rail, and a dirty cowboy hat was jammed on her head. Sitting beside the boots was her third beer of the morning to celebrate the nation's birthday. Below her the scene unfolded like a halting home video. The parade had straggled by—old paunchy men on horseback, an out-of-step bunch of kids posing as a band, a lot of aide cars and fire trucks with their lights whirling and horns blaring. A raggedy assortment of floats was now gathered in front of the library. She could hear the announcer on the crackling public address system, promising to name parade winners very soon. Sun seeped through the umbrella, and sweat trickled under her long-sleeved shirt.

Jenny had been in the Jemez Mountains for two months, following a long-ago memory awakened by watching, of all things, an old John Wayne movie. The red rocks of Monument Valley had reminded her of the red rocks Maria had described when she talked about her New Mexico home. So, Jenny had come with no job and $500 cash in her pocket—and got lucky. The Baca Ranch had just lost a hand, and she was hired in time to herd cattle onto summer range. Today was her first day off since she started work, and she was ready to cut loose. She had dressed in her best jeans, and, at the last minute, put on the belt with the rodeo championship buckle.

She signaled for another beer and watched people wandering around the plaza stopping at booths filled with jewelry, dream catchers, pottery, the usual. Whoa, there was a figure that looked familiar. Could she have had too many beers already? It looked like Maria. She knew that Maria had spent much of her childhood here but years ago had declared her intention never to return. As she watched the woman turn away, Jenny recognized a familiar toss of the head, a well-known swish of blonde hair. No question. It was Maria Swenson. Jenny hadn't seen her in—what—-eight or nine years? Not a pleasant memory. Jenny had acted like an asshole, and she regretted it now, like she regretted most of her actions in the past. Jenny had never apologized to Maria. To others, yes. But not Maria. Maybe now was the time. Maybe after one more beer she would go find her. She watched Maria cross the plaza in the direction of the Bath House and stop as her path was blocked by a woman dressed all in black.

Serafina de Silva had left the Bath House after settling Amelie Jameson, a client she knew from previous visits, in the last empty tub. She had only a few minutes to grab some lunch and get back to work, but she had to get away. Her feet hurt, her back hurt, her fingers hurt from hitting cash register keys. She had called to the other attendant, busy in the back room, that she was going to the bar to pick up her lunch. These holidays created a rage she could barely control—all these strangers in the valley. Yes, it was good for business, as the local business association liked to say, but every one of these tourists was treading on sacred ground. *Her* sacred ground.

Sprinkled among the tourists were locals, many of whom she'd known all her life. "Hi, Virginia. Hi, Boyd. How are you, Mrs. Sandoval. Oh, Nicholas, you're so big now." Hi, hi, hi. She kept smiling and greeting, but her steps never slowed. The bar was full, inside and on the deck, and she stepped around a woman who refused to take her feet off the rail. She grabbed the styrofoam box waiting for her, dropped some bills on the counter and turned to retrace her path. She planned to eat in the shade behind the Bath House, hoping no one would look for her there.

Skirting the line at the BBQ wagon, Serafina came face to face with her worst enemy. Familiar feelings rose inside. Even worse than the outsiders who plagued her were those who had lived here but not honored their families and their land. Especially those *rubias*, blondes, always causing trouble. Her smile turned on again, and her placid voice betrayed none of her inner fury, "Hello, Maria. Having fun?"

She watched those weird-colored eyes shining, that lipstick-red mouth moving, and she tuned out the reply. She'd heard it all before anyway—how spiritual it was here, how restored Maria felt when she came back home. Blah, blah, blah. Of course, Serafina had already known that Maria was back. News traveled fast in a small community. Keeping her mask of polite interest in place, Serafina again began walking in the direction of the Bath House. She felt like dropping her lunch and putting her fingers in her ears. This woman —this hippie —never stopped talking! But she, Serafina, could do something about that. Once the whole village knew Maria for what she was, everyone would see that Serafina was right. She mumbled under her breath as Maria, talking over her shoulder and obviously unaware that the woman in black was not listening, preceded her into the Bath House.

≡ CHAPTER 3 ≡

Amelie heard the screams right after Serafina's soft voice said, for the second time, "Maria, your time's up." Within seconds, chaos erupted. Amelie jumped from the oversize tub, jerked from dreamtime. She was swiping at her pink steaming body with a towel when the curtain enclosing her tub was thrown back. Serafina's eyes were wild. "Are you all right? You're all right, aren't you?" she cried.

"I'm fine. What's wrong?" Amelie answered, struggling to pull clothes over her damp body. "What's going on?" But the woman had moved on to check the next tub, leaving open the curtain to the rest of the room.

Amelie grabbed her daypack and looked out of the tub enclosure. A group of women clustered in the aisle between the tables and the tubs. She could see tangled blonde hair straggling from the head of a figure on the floor, water flowing from the long curls in tiny rivulets across the cement. Already, another woman was performing CPR. Amelie recognized her as one of the massage therapists; she thought her name was Jasmine. Someone was sobbing and repeating, "Oh my god. Oh my god." A voice yelled over and over, "Call 911." Another voice replied each time, "Done. Serafina just ran over to the marshal's office." Jasmine continued her rhythmic movements: breathing into the wet mouth, pushing on the diaphragm.

Amelie, who kept her CPR up to date, pushed forward. "Can I help?" Jasmine didn't pause but exhaled the words when she pushed, "Not yet." With the next push, she breathed, "Help coming." The limp body never stirred except with the ministrations of her would-be savior. The eyes stared up into a void. Amelie knew the woman was dead, knew that Jasmine was working in vain. She glanced around the room. A woman wrapped in a towel helped those enveloped in blankets to disentangle themselves. The high-ceilinged room sweltered, the soothing healing atmosphere displaced by fear and bewilderment.

All the tubs were filled to the brim with steaming water. Amelie stepped nearer to the tub from which the dead woman had been dragged, trying to see an indication of what had happened. A trail of water showed where she had been pulled along the floor. She noted an empty paper cup on the shelf next to the tub. Amelie had welcomed the cool water that Serafina had brought her in a similar cup. A jumble of gold and silver jewelry lay next to the cup. The victim must have removed her jewelry before her bath.

Amelie looked over at the body. The chin was tilted up to clear the airway. She saw an angry red line where a necklace might have been and a faint glimmer of gold chain through the constant motion of CPR. My god, she thought, is that embedded in her neck? With a start, she realized she was looking at the body of the woman who had talked to her so familiarly in the park earlier. At that moment, an EMT in uniform burst through the knot of sweating women, who had clustered in various stages of undress around the drama of life and death. One of them was sobbing continually; another was edging toward the door.

"Hey, Jas," said the newcomer. "Let's get some room. Okay, everyone," she said, addressing the crowd. "Please move into the back room. We need to work here." She knelt awkwardly in the cramped space,

Amelie took the cue and with arms outspread, as though herding a flock of sheep, started moving them through a doorway to a wide corridor, lined with doors opening into small massage rooms. She felt her breath coming hard and inhaled deeply to calm down. Her training persona took over, and she found her voice, ordering the group to move to the next room. An outside door at the end of the corridor was just closing behind someone as she finally got them all corralled. Amelie saw a stocky silhouette in a cowboy hat and wondered what a man was doing on this side of the Bath House.

Amelie zeroed in on the sobbing woman. "Come in here," she said, pushing open a door that revealed a massage table. She helped the woman to sit and stood by her, hand on her shoulder. "Take some slow deep breaths," she advised.

Amelie noticed a bedraggled-looking young woman, shivering in a cotton sundress that looked several sizes too large, who had just reached for the old-fashioned brass knob to the door leading outside. She was debating whether to intercept her or to stay with the still-hysterical woman when the door burst open. Carlton strode in, brown uniform bristling with the usual harsh accouterments: badge, gun, handcuffs, baton, radio. Looking tough and alien among the covey of damp, half-dressed women, he scoped the room and spied Amelie.

"What the hell's going on?" He was all business now, showing no hint of their personal conflict.

"Someone may have drowned. They're doing CPR in there." She jerked her head over her shoulder. He pushed through the group, brushing aside the plucking hand of a woman clutching a towel around her ample hips. "I need my clothes," she said plaintively.

Carlton disappeared into the tub room, and Amelie wondered what to do next. He immediately came back through the door, bending to clear the low jam. "Amelie, could you give me a hand."

"Sure. What do you need?" she asked and stepped closer to him, not looking forward to seeing again the limp naked body stretched out in the next room. She felt huge relief when he said, "Please take these ladies' names and phone numbers. Someone will have to talk to them later."

Amelie nodded. "I think some have left already, but I'll talk to those who are here." She had started to shiver, even though the room was hot and humid. Having a task would allay the shock.

"Right. Thanks." He raised his chin to call out to someone behind him. "Be right there." A brief pat on her shoulder, and he returned to his duties.

Amelie found a notepad on a desk and did a quick tally in her head: all four tubs had been full; three women had been having wraps; and it appeared all three massage rooms had been occupied. That was nine women, plus the girl in the faded old dress, who seemed to have disappeared. And, the thought surfaced in her consciousness again, a man—no, a person—wearing a cowboy hat who had left. She started with the now-quiet woman on the massage table, recording her name, address and phone number. She resisted the impulse to ask other questions like, did you see anyone when you heard the screams? Carlton or the county sheriff's deputies would have to do the investigating.

All of the women had found something to cover their naked bodies, although those who had been soaking or having wraps still had no access to their belongings. In answer to their queries, she opted for the plain truth. "Of course, we'll have to wait for official word, but I'm afraid she is dead." She left them there with the intention to go outside, walk around the Bath House and come in the front door, the only way to avoid passing the body. That way she could reach the men's side and see if anyone was left there who would give her his name.

She was brought up short by the sound of pounding, someone hammering and howling as though from the depths of hell.

"No. No. She can't be dead. She can't be. She's mine. Mine!"

CHAPTER 4

Carlton looked around the tub where the woman had apparently drowned. He already had a sickening feeling that this wasn't an accident, because he had immediately seen the mark on her neck, a deep cut that couldn't possibly have been self-inflicted or accidental. He wished the county would arrive, but the Fourth was a busy day in every jurisdiction. He was reaching for an object that had fallen into a corner behind the plastic chair when he heard a man shouting from the tiny hall separating the two sides of the bathhouse. The door leading to the women's area shook with the rhythmic beating from someone's fists; howls reverberated in the tiny space.

Carlton jerked open the door, and a short well-muscled man practically fell into the room. Instantly, the marshal pinned the raging man's arms behind his back and forced him into the hallway, away from the sprawled body and the two emergency workers. "You can't go in there," he said.

The man pulled one arm free. "Let me go, you bastard." He twisted and kicked at Carlton, knocking over a mop bucket and spreading a film of soapy water over the concrete.

"Goddammit," Carlton growled. "Now I have to get my pants wet." He wrestled his assailant to the floor, and reached back for the handcuffs attached to his belt. The man writhed and twisted, wriggling away like a giant frantic worm. As Carlton attempted to lock the handcuffs, the man heaved with all his strength, and his head smashed into a sharp corner of the concrete steps. He slumped instantly, and a small trickle of bright blood shone through the matted blonde hair and dripped onto the soapy floor.

Carlton looked up to see that a crowd had now gathered in the doorway that led to the lobby, a phalanx of faces all looking horrified. "Oh, shit," he said, imagining the accusations of police brutality sure to issue from the gaping spectators. He saw Amelie attempting to push through the cluster of people. "Let her through," he shouted at the crowd. When Amelie emerged, he motioned her into the small space. "Shut the door behind you!"

Carlton raised himself to one knee, propping his hand on pants that were indeed sopping wet. "Come here with your kit," he yelled to the EMT who stood in the other room beside the now sheet-covered body. "Someone else needs you."

Shit, he said this time to himself. I need some help here. His two deputies were in their cars on the highway, stopping speeders, occasionally cruising at a crawl through the plaza to scoop up anyone who was really, really drunk. He hadn't radioed them after Serafina ran into his office shrieking hysterically because he hadn't thought it would be this serious. One of the county cars should be cruising Highway 4, and he needed to request assistance. Now, the situation was already out of control, and he had no backup.

The EMT had swiftly assessed the man on the floor, who now seemed to be trying to sit up. "He's okay, I think. He'll have a goose egg on his head, but I don't think he's concussed." She taped a gauze pad over a lump already forming.

Amelie stood pressed against the broom closet, looking questioningly at the disparate trio. Carlton seemed to be trying to wring out the hem of his trousers. The handcuffed man sat on the bottom step, his bandaged head drooping. The EMT stood by observing all with complete lack of expression.

"Carlton, what do you want me to do?" Amelie asked.

Carlton lifted his cap to brush back his unruly dark hair, turning his head from side to side as though the answer would materialize in the air. "I don't know." He gestured to the EMT. "She says the victim was long gone when she got here. Then this guy went nuts. I haven't even called the county yet. People are watching like this is a damned TV show. How am I supposed to handle this?"

Amelie knew violent death was uncommon in Cañon Springs; the police dealt with little beyond domestic disputes, juvenile delinquency and traffic offenders. "I'll walk over to your office and leave this list on your desk. You call the county and a deputy." She tilted her head toward the man on the steps. "What are you going to do with him?"

Carlton looked at the EMT. "Can he walk? Does he need a doctor?"

"I think he's okay." She squatted in front of the man. "I advise you to see a physician if you feel dizzy or nauseous. Don't go to sleep for a few hours. Ask someone to check your eyes in about an hour. If your pupils are not the same size, go immediately to a hospital. Got that? Know anyone here?"

He looked up. "Yeah, yeah. Okay, I got it. I feel fine. I know some artists here – Harold, Walter. Yeah, I was just talking to Walter."

It was Carlton's turn to squat in front of the man. "What's your name?"

After a brief hesitation, the man answered. "Sage Hansen."

"Why did you get so upset?"

"Because that's Maria in there. She can't be dead! You got her covered up!" He was twisting again, straining toward the now-closed door where the body lay.

Carlton stood and blocked the door. "Okay, take it easy. I want to talk to you later. I'm going to take these handcuffs off in a minute. You going to stay calm?"

No answer.

"I can't uncuff you until you convince me you're going to walk quietly to the marshal's office and wait for me there."

"Okay, man, I'll go."

Carlton unlocked the cuffs. Amelie said to the seated man, "Come on. I'm a friend of Walter's. I met you earlier, remember? Let's go over to the cop shop. You can sit down there and rest some more."

He looked up and his eyes appraised her in the same way he had earlier, sweeping from breasts to crotch and back to breasts. He must feel better already, she thought.

"Yeah. I remember you." Sage struggled to his feet. "Okay, let's go."

Once inside the marshal's office, Sage could not sit down. He paced from door to window, seemingly unable to rest. The sparse furnishings provided little comfort, consisting of a desk, a computer station, two desk chairs, a table with a coffee maker and four yellow molded plastic chairs for visitors. Amelie sat in one of the chairs, fluffing her still-damp hair. "How does your head feel?"

"Terrible. Hurts like hell." He dropped into the chair next to her and cautiously felt the bandaged lump. "I wanted to talk to her, make her understand. They told me at the Bath House to come back after her bath. So I went to the bar with this guy I know." He jumped up to look out the window again. "Someone ran into the bar and said a woman had drowned at the Bath House. And I wanted to be sure she was okay." He was talking so fast the words ran together. "And there she was. On the floor." He shook his head, winced and sat again.

"She was a girlfriend?" Amelie asked.

"More than a girlfriend." He spoke the word with disdain. "We were together."

Amelie crossed to the coffee maker and poured a cup. She raised it toward Sage. "Want some?"

He paused in his pacing and looked at her as though he couldn't hear well. "What?"

"Something to drink?"

He nodded, and she poured another cup of what smelled like very old coffee. She knew she shouldn't just leave him here, as much as she wanted to go change her clothes and have a stiff drink. Not only had he taken a nasty fall, but Carlton or the sheriff would have to question him about the dead woman. She realized she too would be questioned and also looked out the window. No sheriff's or marshal's deputies in sight. These annual celebrations were a nightmare for the miniscule force because for twelve hours the population of the village increased tenfold. No doubt they had been writing a citation on the highway and were struggling through the traffic to answer Carlton's call.

She turned to Sage. "So, where are you from?"

He resumed pacing, full coffee cup in hand, and she followed his movements with her head like a spectator at a tennis match. "I live in Seattle. I live there with Maria. She used to live around here somewhere but she never talked much about that. I think she has an aunt or a cousin or . . ." His voice trailed off. He put the cup on the desk and raised his fists to either side of his head.

Amelie was afraid he might begin pounding on something like he had in the Bath House. She was a strong woman, but she knew she couldn't restrain him if he started tearing the place up or decided to take off. He walked toward the door but instead of leaving, he stopped and leaned his forehead against the door jamb. His shoulders shook, and she heard the sobs.

Overcoming the distaste she felt at touching him, she gently grasped his arm and led him to a chair then patted his back awkwardly. "It's okay. Let it out." As she spoke the trite phrase, she thought it sounded like a line from a soap opera.

Sage suddenly relaxed, as though his muscles had lost all tension. Turning his head on the table, he closed his eyes and breathed lightly as though he had instantly fallen asleep. Amelie immediately shook his shoulder. "Hey, you can't go to sleep."

He raised his head and smiled beatifically. "Don't worry. I'm okay." His voice was soft but clear. She saw that his pupils looked normal. The sudden change from near manic activity to complete indolence puzzled her. She was reminded of a child who starts having a tantrum then forgets what it was about and falls asleep.

She sat opposite him, sipping the terrible coffee, when a county deputy came through the door. "This the murder suspect?"

CHAPTER 5

The Krazy Kokopelli Bed and Breakfast sprawled at the edge of the river, a typical old New Mexico adobe that had been expanded by the original owners, who had haphazardly added rooms as their family grew. The B&B was Lena's baby. Once Walter had finished renovating the rundown house, he had turned the operation over to his wife. His days were spent in his glass studio.

From the patio, Amelie watched a dipper hop from rock to rock, bobbing into the rippling water for insects. The KK's five rooms were all full, and Amelie could see Lena straightening up the living room. She knew without a closer look that each pillow would be in place, each travel guide aligned on the table. Lena never stopped until the B&B was as perfect as a magazine picture.

Walter came out holding a beer in each hand. He gave one to Amelie and dropped onto a lounge chair, the ever-present pipe clenched between his teeth. They watched an orange glow from the setting sun move up the east side of the valley. A bright strip narrowed as the sun dropped behind the west mesa rim until only one great sandstone prominence glowed as though in a spotlight. Amelie had watched the sun rise and set over the years she had been coming here, tracking its lateral movement through the seasons. At summer solstice, a brightening started early in the morning between two rocks she had named the Mouse Ears. By the shortest day of the year, the sun swung surprisingly far north to rise from behind a little mesa, no longer lighting her favorite room.

Two guests, a young couple, sat at the far end of the patio, murmuring with heads close together. Amelie had heard the front door open and close a few minute ago and assumed that other guests had gone to their rooms. A familiar slap of sandals on the flagstones behind her signaled that Lena was finished inside for a few minutes. The thin woman settled gracefully on another lounge chair with a cup of coffee in hand, flinging back her waist-length black hair. "Okay, tell me. What happened?"

Amelie complied. "A woman drowned in the Bath House while she was having a soak. She actually was in the tub next to me." She paused and sipped her beer. "She came up to me in the park before I went into the Bath House. Just started talking like she had known me forever. Anyway, Serafina found her when her time was up. Everyone went nuts, of course. Carlton came, but he doesn't know what to do with what might be a murder. His roughest cases

17

are rounding up the kids who break into vacation homes."

Walter reached out to lay his pipe in a giant ashtray. "Yeah, Carlton wanted to be anywhere but in the middle of that mess."

Amelie continued. "Jasmine was there and started CPR, and an EMT came right away, but I'm sure she was dead when they pulled her out of the tub. I'm not sure she died from drowning either. She had a wound around her neck." She shuddered. "Someone hurt her."

Lena's black eyes darted between the two. "So, who was she?"

Walter, who hadn't seen the body, gestured to Amelie to continue the story. "A guy who claimed to be her boyfriend said her name was Maria. Said she had relatives here. She looked about 30, long blonde hair, kind of – Hey, he told me she was from Seattle. Think you know her, Lena?"

Lena looked up with a sharp intake of breath and hesitated, lifting her shoulders with a quick jerk. "Seattle's a big place, even when I lived there, which was 15 years ago." Amelie noticed her voice was pitched higher than normal. "Go on. What else?"

Walter picked up the tale. "I went over there when I saw all the excitement. Everybody's crowding around trying to get a look. Ghouls, all of them. Finally, a county deputy comes, and Carlton, looking like he'd been rescued from hell, comes out to tell everyone to go away. Then, an ambulance comes and takes her out the back door. All the women get to put their clothes on. That's it so far."

Lena stared at him. "That's it? That's it? Someone was murdered here! That isn't it. This is . . ." She jumped up and emptied the ashtray into a wastebasket at the far end of the patio. "I can't stand this. Why do people insist on dying here in our peaceful valley. Why would someone do this? We've got to find out who she is."

Amelie and Walter watched her pacing and exchanged looks that silently acknowledged the irrationality of these comments. Lena extended her domain beyond the walls of her home and business to the whole valley. She wanted everything, and everyone, to be as tidy as her living room.

Walter caught his wife's hand as she brushed a leaf off a chair. "*We* don't have to do anything. It'll turn out to be some domestic violence thing."

Lena twined her fingers with his and sat again, but a small line between her straight black eyebrows showed she was not calmed by this assessment. Amelie was aware that Lena was on the verge of saying something more. She could almost see her friend sorting through her thoughts to find one she could voice. Instead, Lena changed the subject. "Carlton coming over tonight?"

Amelie took a last swallow of beer. "I doubt it. He's not too happy with me right now. And he'll probably have to do some work on this for the county."

Lena relaxed a thin increment. "So, you told him, huh?"

Walter stopped refilling his pipe. "Told him what?"

Lena ignored him. "Well?"

Amelie explained to Walter. "I told him I wanted this —us —to be less intense, that I wanted to back off. He didn't take it well. Didn't say anything. Just stopped talking entirely." She threw up her hands. "He wants to be serious. I didn't think he'd be so conventional."

"Amelie," Walter said. "I tried to tell you. He's always been that way. Straightest of the straight arrows." Although Walter had not been born in the valley, his family had come when he was five. He and Carlton had grown up together.

"You told her. I told her." Lena stood with hands on hips, signaling the futility of trying to tell Amelie anything. "Come on, Am. Help me cut up fruit for breakfast." Amelie, recognizing this as a sign Lena wanted to talk to her alone, followed her into the house. At last she would find out why she had been summoned. A guest in the TV lounge greeted them briefly and returned his attention to the screen.

The two women passed the free-standing fireplace into the open kitchen. Lena's breakfasts were half the reason people came to the KK, lavish spreads of fresh fruit, pastries, breads, and the best coffee in the valley. Amelie had been Lena's prep cook many times before, and she found a knife while her friend placed cantaloupe and honeydew melons on the counter. She was a terrible cook and spent more time in Lena's kitchen than her own.

"Carlton is nice, Lena, so nice that I'm getting bored. Can't you find an equally nice woman to divert him in some other direction away from me?" She dumped melon rinds into the garbage disposal. "But we're not going to talk about me. Why did you want to see me?"

Lena didn't answer. Her small heart-shaped face was drawn and pale.

Amelie studied her friend. "Something happened. Before this death. That's why you wanted me to come today."

"Yeah." Lena stopped her work and leaned into the counter. "The truth is I did know a blonde Maria in Seattle, who once lived in New Mexico. Problem is, so did Jenny."

"Okay. What of it?" Amelie spoke casually, but she knew they were entering dangerous territory. Friendly, gregarious Lena had her life in order.

She loved her husband of five years, she loved her business, and she worked like a maniac to eliminate any disruptions. Jenny was the ghost of the past ever present in Lena's nightmares.

"Jenny came here this morning. She wasn't drunk. She didn't hit me. But she's here and wanted to let me know. She got a job up on the Baca, back to being a cowgirl."

Amelie dropped the knife and pounded her fist on the counter. Jenny was a threat. "What was she doing here anyway? I thought you told her to stay away from you. Legally, she *has* to stay away from you. What's she want now?"

Lena grabbed Amelie's clenched fist. "Shh. Walter will hear. No, none of that. She wanted to apologize. Insisted on apologizing. I didn't even let her inside. She was so intense, so insistent about her apology, even that sounded like a threat."

Lena was now cutting a scalloped edge on the watermelon half, but she gripped the knife as though ready for an attack. "That was this morning. Then I hear someone is murdered. And it's too much coincidence. A woman Jenny and I both knew in Seattle was named Maria. A blonde woman, Maria Swenson."

Amelie stopped her work to face her friend. "Are you saying the dead woman is the same Maria?"

"It could be, Amelie. Was she wearing a gold necklace with a little charm like a woman's head on it?"

"Maybe. She was wearing four or five necklaces when I saw her in the park. There was a pile of gold and silver chains with pendants next to the tub where she was killed. And, something was imbedded into her neck when I saw her body." She shuddered as the image appeared in her mind's eye.

Lena clapped her hands over her ears. "Don't tell me any more about that. I can't stand it! I'm just afraid it might be the same Maria." She closed her eyes and massaged her temples. "God! I have the worst headache."

"Not surprising." Amelie looked closely at her friend. "There's more. C'mon, what else?"

Lena sighed. "Okay. I was there. Must have been just before it happened. I drove up to see the parade, but it was so crowded I couldn't get close. I decided to run into the Bath House to drop off some more brochures. Everyone was busy, so I just left them on the counter and decided to come home."

"You must have come in while I was soaking," Amelie said.

Lena shrugged. "No one was at the front desk. Settling people in their tubs, I guess. No one was there at all for the couple of minutes I waited."

"You know you have to tell the sheriff." Amelie was adamant. "At least tell Carlton."

Lena's dark eyes flashed up to Amelie, defiance and pleading mixed in her look. "No. I won't tell anyone. Maybe no one remembers seeing me. I don't want Walter to ever know what happened back then. I was stupid and young and high all the time when I was with Maria and Jenny. And I sure as hell don't want Jenny mad at me for any reason. Please don't tell Carlton, Amelie."

"Lena, are you sure? Of course, I won't say anything if you don't want me to, but this could be serious. I just can't understand why you won't tell Walter."

"Oh, you know. I thought I would at the right time. But that time never came. Then I just let it go." Her voice trailed off. She rubbed her temples and forehead again, then looked back at Amelie. "Promise you won't tell either of them."

Even as she gave her promise, Amelie was pushing back doubts. But what else could she do? Lena had confided only in Amelie about her life before she came to the Jemez, as Lena and other locals called this area. Here, she was a respected business owner, married to a long-time resident—a position being threatened by a crazy woman who meant nothing to her anymore. Amelie returned to cutting fruit, thinking how easily lives can be overturned.

She had been the instrument of overturning more than a few lives herself. And here she was again, wreaking havoc in another. Carlton was a really nice man, so nice that he hadn't recognized she was just having fun. Having sex wasn't supposed to mean she would pledge undying love or get engaged or anything like that. But she finally had to acknowledge an old-fashioned streak in Carlton. He didn't have sex just for fun. He wanted it to *mean* something.

Her thoughts drifted to happier times. She and Carlton had fished cold streams in high country meadows and slept on the cushiony duff of ponderosa pine needles. She had been the one to run forward yelling and clanging a spoon on the coffee pot when a black bear hadn't moved away from their campsite quickly enough. He had showed her a secret hot springs that he had found in his teens. He had been her buddy—and an ardent lover —a perfect relationship to her way of thinking.

This reverie was interrupted when Walter came in to announce the grill was ready for the hamburgers. Lena gave Amelie the look that meant *don't say a word* and swiped plastic wrap over her fruit creation. Amelie carried a tray of condiments out to the patio, looking forward to a traditional Fourth of July meal of beer, burgers, potato salad and watermelon. She treasured these family meals—family meaning Lena, Walter and a few other close friends. When she was growing up, there were no holiday traditions and few meals which her parents shared with her and her brother.

During dinner, they deliberately avoided talking of the murder. Amelie promised again to start researching the history of the 25 acres surrounding the Krazy Kokopelli. She felt guilty about procrastinating on something important to Lena, who had asked for this favor months ago. Amelie had found a million excuses not to drive the 50 miles from Los Alamos to the county seat in Bernalillo to dig through old land records. Lena was paying her in free lodging whenever she came to the Jemez, and no greater proof of their deep friendship could be found than the fact that Amelie had a free room on one of the busiest weekends of the year.

The kitchen conversation with Lena ran as background in Amelie's mind while they ate. Something was still missing. She thought she had heard all about Lena's life in Seattle. Her friend had definite cause to be afraid of Jenny. The abuse had escalated until one night Lena ended up in the hospital. There was a good reason for that restraining order. But she sensed something was still hidden.

The women had been friends for a little more than five years, having met when Amelie was one of Lena's first customers at the Krazy Kokopelli. They had felt an instant affinity for one another, which deepened as they spent long afternoons talking and learning about the parallels in their life stories. Both had been essentially on their own since age 17, albeit from markedly different family backgrounds. Lena had grown up among Kiowa tribal members in the small town of Carnegie, Oklahoma, bouncing throughout childhood from her mother to her aunt to her grandmother. Amelie's family had lived in St. Louis; her parents were quintessential academics, living in their ivory towers. Amelie and Lena had left home and floundered around, again in different ways, before getting their lives on track. They shared an intensity about their work, fueled by the financial vagaries of the self-employed. They also shared the insecurities of children who had been ignored or neglected.

In the kitchen again after dinner, scene of so many intimate revelations, Amelie said, "I think you know more about this Maria, don't you?

Lena sagged against the refrigerator, finally releasing the effort of holding up her facade. She covered her face with both hands, and Amelie leaned forward to hear the muffled words. "She and I were lovers very briefly. Years ago. Another lifetime. Before I met Jenny. Maria is – was – a real 60s throw-back. Moved from one person to another, man or woman, always stayed friendly, loving everyone in that cloying New Age way that makes you want to puke. For her, it was a philosophy of life. For me, it was 'party hearty'." She made quotation marks with her fingers. "I rarely remembered anything I'd done the next day. I knew she had been born in New Mexico, but I never dreamed it was right here."

She dropped her hands and looked at Amelie, eyes glistening with tears. "After we split up, she had a little thing with Jenny. As you know, Jenny never lets go easily. She made threats to kill her, same as she made to me when I left. I don't know, Am, if she'd ever follow through, but I'm afraid — and selfish. I'm afraid I'll get caught up in a scandal. Isn't that awful? I don't care about justice, about truth. It's the worst small town cliché. I'm afraid of a scandal."

CHAPTER 6

Jenny was in line at the Walatowa Convenience Store, holding paper trays of fried chicken and taquitos. The store, operated on tribal land by Jemez Pueblo, sat next to Highway 4 across from what locals called the Red Rocks, an amphitheater of startlingly red sandstone that literally glowed at sunset. It was lunch time, and pizza slices and chicken were selling as fast as the gas at the four pumps outside. People sought shade at picnic tables or leaned against pickup trucks eating take-out from the store or from the row of stands where Pueblo families sold oven bread and enchiladas. In the crowded parking lot, Jenny's Dodge Ram pickup was distinguished by the steer horns mounted on the hood.

Shuffling toward her turn at the cash register, she watched people come and go through the double glass doors, crowding between aisles packed with videos, junk food and soda displays. A young couple in black leather jackets clanking with chains and spikes entered, and she wondered how they could stand that gear in this heat. The girl wore black lipstick and an old cotton sundress under her jacket. Her hair was spiked up with some kind of goo, a purple streak from front to back. His shaved head had a five o'clock shadow. The ring in his nose vied for space with angry red pimples, and, Jenny flinched when she noted this, he had pierced his tongue. Both had tattoos on their knuckles that Jenny didn't even want to know about.

Several more customers crowded into the store and greeted friends. Boxed pizza slices vanished from under the heat lamps and were replaced in a blur. Four tattooed hands grabbed a box each. Then Jenny saw them leaving, walking swiftly toward an old Ford station wagon parked by the front door.

"Hey," Jenny called to the dark-haired woman who was making change and swiping credit cards. "Those two just stole some pizza." The woman flicked a glance at Jenny and yelled for someone to come up front.

Jenny's temper flared. She ran out, still holding her food, which brought the manager, an older Jemez man, right behind her.

"Excuse me, ma'am. Did you plan to pay for that?"

"Me! Pay? Did you hear me? It's those kids who stole something. Not me."

"What kids?"

Jenny turned and saw a plume of black smoke swirl down the highway.

"Never mind. They're gone now. Don't you have any security?"

The man shrugged. "Saw you, didn't we?"

Jenny thrust her food into his hands. "Here. Forget it. I'm not hungry." She stalked to her truck, tossed her cowboy hat onto the seat, and raced out of the parking lot, not pausing at the stop sign before she turned north on Highway 4.

Ignoring the speed limit, she caught up with the battered green Ford just as it turned off the highway. Well, if no one else cared, she'd bust the little fuckers. Scare them, anyway. Plus, they'd made her miss her lunch.

The smoking station wagon bounced over ruts and rocks as it climbed. In a mile, it turned onto a fainter dirt road and rolled to a stop beneath the bluffs that rose to Cat Mesa.

Jenny pulled up beside them, jumped out and jerked open the driver's door.

"I saw you steal that pizza," she yelled into the boy's face.

"Yeah, so." His shock turned to a sneer, and he thrust himself out of the car and up against Jenny.

She held her ground, smelling his sour breath and seeing close-up the blackheads in his pale unhealthy skin. He raised one hand and Jenny braced herself for a blow, but he placed his hand on her chest and shoved, forcing her to step back to regain her balance.

Jenny exploded, bringing a fist up to smash into his face. Blood spurted from his nose, and Jenny hit him again in the same place, hearing a solid pop as his nose broke. She had no fear of this pseudo-tough guy, who was close to her height and as soft as a marshmallow. She regularly tossed bales of hay, castrated calves and mended fence. From the time she could walk, she had defended herself against two older brothers. In fact, this little fucker reminded her of the younger of the two, whom she had once feared for his sneak attacks.

The girl came around the station wagon, screaming. "Stop it. What's the matter with you?"

Jenny had pulled her arm back to punch again, but paused to look at the frantic young woman.

"You're next. You're both thieves. Snotty little brats."

The girl retreated. Then, apparently thinking she was at a safe distance, started screaming over and over: "Stop it! Stop it!"

"Shut up, Ellie," the boy yelled, swiping at his bloody nose and look-ing at his gory hand in disbelief. Taking advantage of Jenny's distraction, he threw himself on her, both of them falling to the ground. His blood smeared on Jenny's sweat shirt.

They rolled in the red dirt like two kids in a schoolyard fight, punching and kicking, mostly hitting the ground or the air. Finally, Jenny pulled free, and with all her weight behind it, landed a jarring punch on his jaw. She followed it by picking up his head and slamming it onto the ground. Stunned, he lay still, his eyelids flickering.

The girl, who finally realized that her protector was getting whipped, jumped on Jenny's back. Jenny easily shrugged her off and stood up, brushing dirt from her jeans and shirt. Her breath came in hard gasps. Dried grass stuck out from her short hair.

"Get out of here, you two." She advanced toward the boy who had staggered to his feet and was backing toward the dilapidated vehicle.

The couple scrambled inside, and the girl defiantly snapped down the door lock. The boy glared through the window. "Bitch. I'll get you."

Jenny returned the look with a cold stare and spit on the ground. He spun the back wheels and shot down the dirt track. A cloud of dust settled over her as she took several deep breaths.

Suddenly, she slumped to her knees. God, what had gotten into her? Beat the kid up over a few slices of pizza. Not even her pizza. The old Jenny felt good to have hit someone, to smash something that released the anger. Her rage burned like a pilot light, always there, waiting to be struck into flame. The new Jenny despaired of ever disciplining herself to substitute new patterns for old. In anger management sessions, the therapist counseled to wait and think of the consequences. Today she hadn't waited. All the emotion of the past week had blasted out like a whirlwind. Good news was there wouldn't be any consequences. No one had seen the fight, and he was unlikely to report her.

She sat in the dirt and stared across the canyon at the opposite rim. Below, green cottonwoods meandered in a fluid line marking the river's path to the Rio Grande. Turning her head to loosen the muscles in her neck, her eye caught a flicker of motion. A rabbit hopped from under a juniper and stopped paralyzed at the sight of a human. She focused on the rabbit, and then noticed a trail in the dirt that looked like something had been dragged. The marks led to a little arroyo where several large junipers had banded together. She followed the track and circled around the junipers. An old canvas tarp, nearly camouflaged by red dirt thrown over it, humped over something the size of a bolster pillow. Rocks held the tarp's edges in place.

Jenny lifted one corner and revealed a black plastic garbage bag, tied with a twisty. She pulled it open and found an assortment of groceries — boxes of sugary cereal, cans of pork and beans, bags of chips and cheese puffs. The chips and cereal looked like a mouse had been at them. Inside a gallon-size plastic freezer bag was the real surprise. She squatted back on her heels. Now she wished she'd done more damage to that little bastard! The baggie contained four watches, six wallets, several tangled necklaces, and numerous pairs of earrings with price tags attached. She was positive this loot had been hidden by the couple she had followed. Obviously, their larceny wasn't limited to food.

She laid the small bag on the ground while she replaced the tarp. The police should have this, but Jenny hated the police. In Seattle, where she'd been taken to King County jail, the officers had subdued her with their sticks when she'd fought her arrest. Once she'd been handcuffed, the older cop, pot belly hanging over his belt, had probed his beefy fingers everywhere when he searched her and kept one hand on her breast when he'd pushed her into the patrol car. Invariably, the officers who had responded to neighbors' complaints of domestic violence had made no effort to hide their disgust at being called to intervene between two female partners.

New Jenny and old Jenny started another argument in her head. Go to the police. Act like a responsible citizen for once. No, the police won't believe me. They'll insult me, probably lock me up for taking this stuff.

Hefting the baggie in her hand, she made a decision and put it back under the tarp. Then she scuffed the dirt and kicked some rocks around to hide her tracks. She hurried to her truck and bumped her way back to the highway. Using the pay phone outside the convenience store, she called the Cañon Springs marshal's office, trying to disguise her voice by putting a bandanna over the receiver, something she'd seen in a movie. "You'll find some stolen jewelry and other stuff on the mesa to the east of the gas station. Turn on Camino Blanco and go for about a mile then turn toward the big mesa. Look for fresh tire tracks. The people who stole it are two punks in leather – boy and girl – driving an old green Ford station wagon that smokes like a chimney. The guy has a broken nose — probably went to the clinic."

She hung up the phone, ran back to her truck and retraced her trail up on to the mesa. She pulled off and hid the truck behind an abandoned single-wide trailer with a couple of rusted out cars on blocks in front. Jumping out, she ran up the road again, skirting the place where the fight had occurred, and found a spot with a view of the tarp. In her experience, the cops would steal anything valuable. She wanted to see if New Mexico law enforcement was any different.

As it turned out, all the running and hurrying were unnecessary. Forty-five minutes later a black Bronco with "Cañon Springs Police" on the door crawled up the road, passed the track, reversed and turned into the right place. A uniformed man walked around the area for a few minutes, collected the tarp and garbage bag, returned to his official SUV and moved at the same stately pace down the road and out of sight.

She rose and stretched her legs, but stayed in the shade. The marshal might decide to come back for some reason, and she didn't want to be in the open if he did. The dust had settled and she had almost decided it was safe, when a familiar vehicle with two occupants came slowly along the road, trailing a plume of dust. The green station wagon had also been in a hiding place, and Jenny had to admit that the kids were smarter than she'd thought. Instead of running to get his nose fixed, the punk had come back to get his loot – or to get her.

CHAPTER 7

Amelie climbed a dusty path to the top of Virgin Mesa, red dirt coating her new Asolo hiking boots and clinging to her bare legs. The week had been hectic. A quick trip to Artesia, another to Chama, she'd been from one end of New Mexico to another. She would have preferred to stay in her little duplex apartment in Los Alamos and not be in the car again for two days, but she was back in the Jemez Valley to hike and to be with Lena.

She had passed up the chance for a day hike with a Russian man whom she'd met at the grocery store, a man with strong, lean legs and a history of hiking twenty miles a day on every vacation. What little she got of his background while they waited in line was that he was at Los Alamos National Laboratory for a year doing post-doctoral work in computer systems engineering. He'd been delighted with the network of trails around Los Alamos and was systematically jogging every one, checking them off a list.

She had thought about bringing Ivan along this weekend—yes, he had a stereotypic Russian name that she thought amusing, like Boris and Natasha in the Bullwinkle cartoons. However, the chance that they might run into Carlton—a high probability in this small community—made that a bad idea. So she was hiking alone several miles downstream from the KK, having satisfied herself last night that Lena was not being harassed by Jenny and that steady business at the KK kept her from brooding.

She scrambled the last steep section of the faint trail, gained the flat top of the mesa, and inhaled the familiar smell of sun-warmed pine needles. Of all the scents on earth, this was her favorite. The aroma was like apple pie, a smell of coming home, of feeling safe. Love of the outdoors was an integral part of the life she had created for herself in New Mexico, a life far different from the stultified atmosphere of her childhood home. Her parents had been academics, immersed in teaching, research and writing. Their idea of an outdoor adventure was loading up on food from the nearest deli and spending a couple of hours in the backyard of their St. Louis home.

Striding up a little arroyo, she stopped when she saw the familiar triangular shape of a pot sherd lying on the ground. In a few steps, she saw several more, dark gray bits of ancient pottery. She strolled on, casting from side to side until she came to a mound strewn with large stones of a fairly even size. Off to one side was a slightly rounded depression with a piñon tree growing in its center. This was a small ruin compared to many in the Jemez

Mountains, long buried under red dirt and centuries' accumulation of forest debris. Archaeologists estimated that these mountains had been home to as many as 30,000 people in the 12th century. Some of the largest archaeological ruins in North America lay atop these mesas. Amalie often wished she had pursued a career in archaeology. However, by the time she had finished her fairly useless B.A. in American Studies, she needed to go to work.

She sat down and pulled a water bottle from her pack, absently fingering a pot sherd and thinking how good the early morning sun felt on her face. She let out a deep breath of relaxation resonating to the sound of the wind soughing through the pines. A brown creeper spiraled up the trunk of a nearby Ponderosa, prospecting for insects in the rough bark. She had brought her journal and, dating a new page, wrote about the birdcalls, the comforting smell and the sure feeling that she had pine sap on the seat of her shorts. She wrote about Carlton, going to a deeper layer of feeling about the many men who had come and gone. This was a recurring theme in the years of notebooks stacked on her closet shelf. She loved men, their particularly masculine smells, their large hands and strong musculature, their singular differentness from women. Each new lover was an adventure into the world of the other, a chance to find a pure connection that resembled the near telepathy she had achieved with a few women friends like Lena. Since she was seventeen, she had been on a quest for the perfect combination of physical and emotional attraction. A few had been close, one she had married, briefly, but the search continued.

In her journal, she questioned herself. Did her idealized relationship even exist in this world? And when she found her many couplings less than ideal, how could she make an exit that didn't cause pain? She just wasn't good at endings, never could find a way to make a clean break. Lost in the familiar and puzzling maze of her inner self, she was aroused by a scuffling sound on the trail she had just ascended.

She put her journal in the pack and stood up, not wanting to surprise or be surprised by another creature, human or otherwise, in this isolated spot. Whatever crunched on the pine needles passed behind a rock outcropping. Slightly nervous now, Amelie called out, "Hello." Immediately, a person appeared, and a woman's voice replied, "Oh, I didn't expect to see anyone here."

Amelie stood up and saw a tiny woman, wearing a loose black blouse and long black skirt and carrying a liter bottle of Mountain Dew. She looked familiar, but it wasn't until she spoke again that Amelie remembered that she worked at the Bath House. Hers was the soft voice that led people to their tubs, checked to see they had enough drinking water, and told them when their time was up.

"I'm used to walking this land alone." The woman shook her head and sunbeams highlighted gray streaks in the smooth black hair. Now Amelie saw that she was older than she had looked at first. The bright light revealed tiny crow's feet spreading from the corners of her eyes, and lines had started to deepen around her mouth. But she moved like a young woman, lithe and quick, with feline grace and strength.

Amelie extended her hand. "I'm Amelie Jameson. I've seen you at the Bath House. You're Serafina, right?"

"Serafina de Silva." She spoke proudly and merely brushed Amelie's palm with her soft hand. "I see you found one of my favorite spots."

An edge to the sweet voice struck a small warning in the back of Amelie's mind. She, too, often felt possessive of places where she liked to meditate or write, places she'd claimed as hers no matter who the legal owner. But she'd better check.

"I'm sorry if I'm trespassing. I just wanted to explore, and I didn't see any signs."

"Oh, no. You're not trespassing. Not on my land anyway." She uncapped the bottle and drank some of the fizzy liquid. "You don't live around here. I know everyone in the valley except the newest people." Her tone implied they weren't worth knowing anyway.

"I live in Los Alamos. I'm staying at the Krazy Kokopelli." Amelie was determined to establish a conversation. "I'm a good friend of Lena's." She noticed some plants in the woman's hand. "Oh, are you picking flowers?" They actually looked like weeds to Amelie. Serafina ignored the question.

"Oh, yes. Lena. A newcomer. She sends a lot of people to the Bath House, and we send a lot of people to her." Serafina's eyes narrowed. They were amber and translucent, like the sun shining through a tiger's eye gemstone.

"How long have you worked there – at the Bath House?" Amelie asked. Something was bugging this woman, maybe annoyance at finding someone where she had hoped to be alone.

"I've been there ten years, but I've lived here all my life. My mother still lives here, and two brothers and cousins and aunts and uncles. I can show you our house." She turned and walked between the thick ponderosa trunks toward the east rim of the mesa.

Amelie followed and asked the question that was really on her mind. "Do they know who killed that woman? You found her, didn't you? That must have been terrible."

Serafina stopped for a moment."Hmmm," she said and walked on. "It's hard to talk about that. She was dead when I found her. No one got arrested yet." She turned. "I know who did it. I told the sheriff, but I haven't heard anything about it."

Now Amelie stopped. "You know who did it? Who?"

"A bum. A dirty boy who lives in a car. I've seen him getting out of it when I drive to work. Earrings and tattoos and who knows what else. He was there, hiding in the men's side of the Bath House where he wasn't supposed to be. Stealing, I bet. Probably his skinny little girlfriend was there, too. One man said $20 was gone from his wallet, and women have complained of lost jewelry. This time, no one blamed us, the attendants. They were too excited about being there for a murder."

They neared the edge of the mesa where broken rock and sandstone bluffs fell away to the valley floor hundreds of feet below. Amelie canted her hip to place a booted foot on a boulder that edged the mesa. She was so surprised by Serafina's revelation that she didn't look at the view. The other woman went on talking as though she hadn't just accused someone of murder. She gestured toward the land below them.

"That's my house, my land."

Amelie shaded her eyes with her hand and tried to see a building below. The meandering line of the river was marked by bright green cottonwoods in the *bosque*. A tiny pickup noiselessly turned off the highway onto one of the many gravel roads that led to houses along the river. Looking up the canyon, she thought she could see the KK roof through the trees.

Amelie squinted. "I can't see a house."

Serafina's eyes were fixed on a spot directly below them. "It's there. Waiting for me. It's always been there. *My* land." She emphasized the possessive pronoun as though Amelie had been arguing with her.

Amelie shifted to follow her outstretched arm and saw a brown rectangle in a clearing, an old adobe that blended almost invisibly into the earth from which it was made. Near it, a scraggly line of fence posts formed a square enclosing a barely visible vehicle sunk into the earth. Nothing moved near the house, which was probably a mile from the main road at the end of a dirt track.

Serafina seemed bemused as she gazed down on the land below them, lost in a personal reverie. A raven flew over them and called twice in its raucous voice.

Amelie did not want to be diverted from the murder. "What did the sheriff say when you told him about this dirty boy?"

"He said he'd look into it. I have heard nothing more."

"Have you talked to Carlton?"

"Carlton." The scorn was evident. "I've known Carlton since we were babies. He can't find a murderer."

Amelie wanted to ask more, but Serafina had folded her arms across her chest and appeared to withdraw from the space she occupied. Amelie had the weird thought that the woman would fade like the Cheshire cat until she disappeared. Maybe only her cat-like eyes would remain. She certainly hadn't smiled, so she wouldn't leave that behind.

Amelie decided it was time for her to move on. She asked, "Do you know if there are any petroglyphs on these rocks? I always look to see if I can find any."

Serafina didn't turn her gaze. "I don't know. I've never tried to find such things."

Amelie didn't believe this for a minute. The old-time families knew every rock for miles around from lifetimes of trips to cut wood and round up cattle. But, she was not surprised that Serafina didn't want to reveal any local secrets. She had already learned that the old families didn't easily tell their stories to newcomers—and that included anyone who hadn't lived here for generations. "I think I'll take a look. Nice talking to you."

Amelie lowered herself between two boulders and scrambled about twenty feet down into an open space where she could turn and inspect the smooth orange sandstone that rimmed the mesa. Immediately, a form caught her eye. On a boulder, just at ground level, was an image—roughly a stick-figure human. Petroglyphs were created by striking stone on stone to chip away the surface and reveal the lighter stone beneath. The lines on this one that formed the angled arms and legs were covered in places with pale green lichen. That meant she had found an old one that had not been touched in generations if lichen had grown into it. She pulled her journal from her pack and squatted to sketch the shape. In the next hour she found three more petroglyphs. One panel depicted a row of deer, one with a smaller deer inside. A pregnant animal, Amelie had read, could represent fertility.

A huge boulder offered a shady spot to eat her lunch of crackers, cheese and apple. Finished eating, she scrambled back up to the mesa top and circled the irregular shape of the ancient pueblo to find the path she had ascended.

Only her footprints disturbed the fine dirt. How had Serafina come up, and where had Serafina gone? She had heard or seen nothing since their conversation – no footsteps, no rockfall, no engine starting.

Her car had baked in the sun for four hours, and Amelie sat with the doors open and the air conditioner on full blast while she pulled off her boots and put on her sandals. She thought again of her meeting with Serafina. The woman had appeared dazed. And then she had disappeared. Well, of course, that was impossible. Maybe there was another trail down.

Back at the main road, Amelie turned to the north, driving in sunlight filtered through cottonwood leaves, the road winding and rising as she continued. She passed scattered houses—old adobes mixed with double-wide trailers. In a couple of miles she saw a dirt track leading off to the left and thought maybe that was the way to the house Serafina had shown her from the mesa. On impulse, she turned. Not that Serafina was all that welcoming. If she's there, I'll just say I'm lost, Amelie thought.

Grass grew high on the mound between the two parallel paths. She maneuvered around potholes and then came to a huge puddle that spanned the track. She splashed through the muddy water only to be stopped by a massive cottonwood limb that blocked the way.

Maybe this wasn't the way to Serafina's house, but it looked worth exploring. Parking the car, she walked along the track, which dropped toward the river. Around a bend, she caught sight of an adobe house—really a ruin—deteriorated by years of weather and intrusions of animals. Vines grew over the walls and twirled through the broken windows. Crumbling plaster revealed old adobes weathering way from years of rain and sun. She peered through a window, long since without glass, its unpainted wood frame warped and pulling away on one side. On the inside wall, a patch of sunlight highlighted a sagging wooden door, partially revealing another room filled with collapsed *vigas*, Ponderosa pine beams cut long ago in the nearby mountains. A hummingbird zipped over her head, and high above a raven called. The roof on one end was completely collapsed under the weight of a giant limb from another hoary cottonwood. This couldn't be Serafina's home. Then she saw the corral, in exactly the relationship to the intact walls as she'd seen from above. Posts made of twisted juniper branches had once held the rusty barbed wire that lay on the ground. In the center of the former enclosure was the rusted shell of a truck, half-buried by decades of drifting silt.

Amelie was sure she was standing in front of the place that Serafina had pointed out. The woman was in a time warp. Only pack rats and snakes made a home here now. She walked back along the track, reviewing their brief conversation. Serafina had claimed this melting pile of adobe was her residence and accused some unknown man of murder. She would ask Carlton what he knew about this story—if he would ever talk to her again.

CHAPTER 8

Dust saturated the marshal's office, rising and settling over every horizontal surface each time a car passed. The small adobe had been a livery stable 150 years ago, when Highway 4 had been a dirt track through the village. Then the road was paved in 1963, and many of the historic buildings in Cañon Springs were suddenly only a few feet from the asphalt's edge. Even the notorious 25 mph speed limit couldn't entirely mitigate the impact of modern traffic on venerable adobe walls.

Amelie sat at the newly installed computer and patiently explained again to the clerk how to enter information on citations issued in the past year. She shifted to release strain on her back and kicked the extension cord that led to one of two outlets in the room. Tami, the young woman hired to do data entry, was trying hard, but Amelie had to draw a picture of every process. Literally. For the third time, she sketched a straggling flow chart of the steps required to find a previously recorded citation should it be requested by the court or law enforcement agencies. "Find the folder named 'traffic'. Click on the alphabetical list . . .." She shook her head, feeling as though the dust in the air had penetrated her brain, awareness of Carlton hovering just beyond the haze.

The marshal sat hunched over his desk at the back of the room, away from the smeared windows, appearing intent on studying the documents before him. The fact that he hadn't turned a page in fifteen minutes told Amelie that he was as distracted as she was. While her pencil made marks on the pad and her mouth voiced instructions, her mind was seething with their last words at lunch.

The day had started well enough. She had arrived in mid-morning, checked that last week's records had been properly entered, and did a demonstration of the retrieval process for Tami, Carlton and his deputies. She insisted that everyone in the office learn the procedures, even though Tami would do all the data entry. When they had finished, to Amelie's surprise Carlton had asked her to lunch at the bar. They had walked the short distance in amiable silence.

The Rio Jemez Bar and Grill liked to style itself as a saloon, and in keeping with that Wild West concept, had decorated the interior with heads of various dead animals and paraphernalia of early ranching days: harness, barbed wire, branding irons. While they waited for their green chile cheeseburgers,

Amelie studied, as she did on each visit, the mountain lion pelt hanging on the wall. The seven-foot-long beast had been shot in the nearby mountains in 1967.

This was the first time Amelie and Carlton had been alone together since the day of the murder, and she was eager for news of the investigation. She turned her attention to her companion and was startled to find his deep brown eyes concentrated on hers. She ignored the plea implicit in that look.

"Do you know who the victim is?" she asked, trying not to sound too interested. She didn't think anyone could connect Lena, but she had to find out for sure.

"Yes, as a matter of fact, I knew her when I was a kid. She lived here off and on until we were in sixth grade."

So he did know her. Amelie wasn't too surprised. This was a very small town. "Then she comes back and gets killed? What's that all about?"

He shrugged. "So far, Sage is the only one we know about who has a connection to her. I mean, other people who grew up here probably remember her, but I don't think anyone else has talked to the deputies."

"What happened to Sage?" she asked.

Carlton took a couple of gulps from a glass of iced tea. "The county guys talked to him for a while, but he said he wasn't even in the Bath House when she died. He had gone in there earlier but she was already in a tub. So he went on over to the bar and heard from somebody there that a woman named Maria had died. And you saw what happened then."

"Who's the person he was talking to?" Amelie asked at the same time she lifted the huge hamburger to her mouth. Green chile dribbled from the bun onto her plate.

"Some Santa Fe artist, who had, of course, left town by the time this came out. I guess they're going to get the Santa Fe police to find him."

"He was pretty weird that day when I took him to your office," Amelie said. "Shock, I guess. First he was hysterical and thrashing around, then like a switch had been turned off, he was calm and quiet, too quiet, like he'd gone to another place in his mind."

"I know. He went crazy at the Bath House, but I didn't see any unusual behavior when he was being interviewed," Carlton agreed. "He seemed rational, reasonable, perfectly at ease. Except for that big lump on his head you'd never know he was the same guy I wrestled with. I haven't seen him since. All that's out of my hands now."

Carlton confessed that he had received a real dressing down from the county sheriff after they had gone over the murder scene. "I focused on the women's side, where the body was. You know, you were there. In fact, they gave me hell for letting you talk to witnesses and allowing you to escort Sage to the office. While all that was going on, the men who had been soaking on the other side just walked out. Serafina checked the appointment book and gave the deputies those names. And somebody thought there had been at least one other person on the women's side, but, hell, anyone could have come and gone in all the confusion, and we'd never know."

Amelie suddenly recalled meeting Serafina on the mesa. "I ran into her when I was hiking last week."

"Who?"

"Serafina, who works at the Bath House, who found the body. She said she went to school with you."

"Yeah. I've known her all my life. Her and her brothers, her cousins, her parents and grandparents. It's a big family, but a lot of them have moved away."

"Where does she live?" Amelie thought of the ruined adobe that Serafina claimed as her home.

"She lives in San Ysidro. The family still has property south of Cañon Springs, but no one lives there now. They once owned quite a bit of land in the valley."

Amelie leaned across her empty plate. "She told me she knows who did it."

"Yeah. Right." If Amelie had expected an excited reaction, she was disappointed. Carlton pushed a couple of fries into his mouth and chewed before responding. "Over the years she has confided to me that she knows who shot through the window of the Presbyterian Church, who stole the painting of the first mayor from the village office, who did God knows what else. She always knows something no one else does, and it always gives her a chance to point a finger at someone she doesn't like. Lately, it's been someone she doesn't even know. She thought she was being followed here each day from San Ysidro. Convinced me. I stopped this poor guy in the car she described. He had just driven here from Texas, never been in the valley before." He drained the last of his iced tea. "What I'm saying is, I wouldn't put too much stock in what Serafina reports."

Amelie nodded. This confirmed her impression of the woman, who had been actually kind of spooky. She didn't bother to tell Carlton about Serafina's report of the "dirty boy."

Carlton pushed his plate aside, cleared his throat and took her hand.

"Amelie, please tell me what I can do. What can I do to make you happy?"

Amelie, surprised by the sudden switch in the conversation, squeezed his hand and pulled hers away. She raised her gaze to study again the tawny lion skin on the wall. Just when she thought they could get away with nothing more than a casual conversation, he had to get serious again.

"Carlton, it's not a matter of making me happy. This is all about me and not about you. And I think I make my own happiness. I–" She faltered. How to explain that she was still grazing, still sampling this man and that? How to not sound so callous and shallow that she'd be embarrassed to say it?

Carlton's jaw tightened, and he pushed his chair back.

She reached out and grasped his forearm. "Carlton, can't you just let it go? We're not a match. It would be wonderful if we were because you're a wonderful man, but–"

He pulled his arm away, rose to his feet, and slapped a couple of bills on the table. Amelie watched him push through the door and finished the sentence in her head, thoughts she had no intention of sharing with him. *The real truth is that I met a man in Los Alamos who interests me.* There. She'd admitted to herself that she was on the move again, musing about phoning a Russian man she'd talked to for ten minutes while waiting in line with her grocery cart.

She checked to see how much money Carlton had left. Even with all this, he'd still bought her lunch. Now, she had to go back to the office and finish her work ten feet across the room from him. Maybe he'd find a sudden need to patrol the highway.

However, when she returned, he had been sitting in his gloomy corner, once more pretending to read. She had immediately recognized the signs of confusion on Tami's face and sat down to draw another diagram. The thick silence of two people trying not to notice each other permeated the atmosphere.

Amelie was putting everything back into her brief case, ready to leave, when a deputy came through the door, pushing two young people before him, clad inappropriately in leather jackets. Amelie noted the young man's grimy neck and blackened fingernails, and his companion's almost emaciated frame. Far from being subdued by officialdom, both were screeching at anyone who came into view.

The boy glared at the deputy. "Why are you arresting me? I got beat up, you dumb shit. I never saw that stuff before. Go find that crazy cowgirl bitch who did this to me." He pointed to his swollen nose.

The girl's shrill complaints rose over his shouts. "Look for the lady with the big belt buckle and the dumb horns on her truck. She's nuts. She came after us. We didn't do nothing."

Her boyfriend said automatically, "Shut up, Ellie."

Carlton came to his feet and motioned the deputy to take the two into the back room, really a large closet where they held those who were to be transported to the county jail. Through the closed door, Amelie could hear the rant continue although she couldn't make out any words. She wanted to tiptoe across the room and lay her ear against the door. Carlton was having none of that. Using his official voice he said, "I think we're through here today." He waited until both Amelie and Tami had gathered their things and left.

Amelie lingered on the porch, ostensibly groping through her purse for car keys. She could hear faint sounds as the two miscreants continued to berate the officers. The brief encounter had set in motion two trains of thought. Serafina had mentioned a dirty boy with earrings and tattoos. Could mean nothing. Lots of kids got pierced and decorated these days. The other thought was more disturbing.

On the winter evening when Lena had revealed the story of her relationship with Jenny, she told Amelie about what she called Jenny's wild west alter ego. In her teens, Jenny had entered a junior rodeo and, competing against the boys, had won the bulldogging. She wore that belt buckle everywhere, Lena said. To top it off, she had mounted steer horns on the cab of her pickup, proving she was a real hick to most of their Seattle friends. Lena had shared convincing examples of Jenny's explosive rages, as well as her equally passionate regrets. If Jenny had assaulted this pair of kids, it must be because she had found some connection to Maria. She wouldn't be slow to avenge her former lover's death, even if they'd been estranged, even if the consequences would be severe.

Amelie struggled to understand her responsibility in the midst of divided loyalties. The boy in custody was obviously the one Serafina had accused of Maria's murder. Amelie had been touched by Carlton's rueful confession at lunch that he had failed to secure the murder scene. She wanted him to prove he could handle this. However, Carlton had made it clear he thought Serafina was spiteful, if not delusional. Her other problem struck deeper. She could identify the woman the young couple claimed had committed assault. Yet, she had promised Lena she wouldn't reveal Jenny's presence, much less her connection to the dead woman. Now Jenny had confronted this boy and his girlfriend. Maybe Serafina was right about their connection to the murder, but how could Jenny know?

With that conundrum to turn over in her mind, she got in her car and started up into the mountains on the road to Los Alamos. She had to think about this some more before making a move that could get Lena into trouble.

CHAPTER 9

Los Alamos didn't appear on maps until the 1960s, even though it had been founded, almost overnight, in 1949, when Robert Oppenheimer selected it as the location for the top-secret Manhattan Project. While the inhabitants went about their lives – shopped for groceries, made love, designed nuclear bombs – they were invisible to the rest of the world. Today the town of 14,000 remains introverted, although maps now show its location. A sense of constraint, of reticence makes a visitor feel that much goes on behind closed doors. The duplexes and fourplexes built for nuclear scientists and their families survive as rental units, and cyclone fences topped with razor wire surround the many units of Los Alamos National Laboratory scattered through the surrounding forest.

Amelie stepped out of her duplex on Walnut Street at 6 am and waved to her neighbor who left for work at the same time each morning. She followed a dusty trail into Walnut Canyon, a small ravine by the standards of the Pajarito Plateau. The high plateau was cut deeply by numerous canyons, leaving thin plateaus like monster fingers spreading to the east as though trying to reach the Sangre de Cristo mountains forty miles away.

Within two minutes of leaving her porch, she had dropped out of sight of houses, although she could hear dogs barking above her in the pines. This was why she loved the location of her apartment, backed up against the canyon. She could pretend she was in the wilderness just a few steps from her door. When she reached the bottom of the steep path, she did her stretching routine and started jogging on her usual route. The shade was already vanishing; by afternoon, the rock around her would be radiating heat from the unrelenting midsummer sun. Her tank top and shorts made her feel a little cool now, but that wouldn't last long.

She caught sight of a huddled figure just as she came to the junction with vast Pueblo Canyon, a mile from her starting point. A man was seated on a rock beside the trail, bent over, his back to her. She slowed, and he turned at the sound of footsteps. With a slight shock, she recognized the man she'd met at the grocery store whom she'd been fantasizing about for a week. Now this was a sign, she thought. She stopped and said, "Hi, Ivan."

He looked closely, then remembered. "Ah. From the market. Good morning," he replied, the Russian accent creating an uncertain rhythm to his speech. "You run early also. Before sun is . . ." He pointed a finger directly overhead.

"Yes, I try to get up early when I'm at home and spend an hour running. Are you resting?"

He laughed, as though resting was an improbable concept in his life. "The shoe . . ." What you say? Broken. I try to fix." He used the same finger to point now at his running shoe, and she saw that he had tied together two ends of a separated shoelace.

"Boy. That doesn't happen much any more, with nylon laces. You must have gotten a lemon." She watched him study her face intently and knew he was mentally translating. As always happened when speaking to those for whom English is a second language, she was suddenly aware of the idioms sprinkled through American speech. *Boy? Lemon?* Literal translations sounded nonsensical.

He straightened and stood. She noticed how very tight his skimpy nylon running shorts were, the bulge in his crotch prominent and, yes, tantalizing. He must have bought them a size too small. She wondered if this was by error or design. The mesh nylon tank top revealed smooth muscular arms and a small thatch of brown hair centered on his chest. She kept her eyes moving, off to the distance up the canyon, so he wouldn't think she was ogling him. However, when she looked at his face again, his direct gaze and slight smile made her think he had just read her mind.

"I think I start again," he said. "Which way do you go? I go with you."

Amelie said, "I usually run to below the airport, then back to my house up there." She gestured behind her. "Ready?"

They jogged in companionable silence for another twenty minutes, Amelie pleased that they moved at a similar pace. At a junction with another canyon, she said, "This is where I usually turn around. Are you going on?"

He paused and appeared to consider the question. "Today I return."

By the time they reached the spot where they had met, both were dripping with sweat, and heat waves were visibly rising from the boulders that lined the canyon.

"My house is right up there." Amelie pointed up to where the sun was lighting the houses on the rim. "Would you like a glass of lemonade?"

He gravely consulted his watch. He appeared to deliberate on each small decision. "I have thirty minutes, then I must go."

Inside her house, Ivan accepted the towel she offered and rubbed his head and upper body. Amelie noticed his biceps harden and relax as he smoothed his short hair. While she mixed frozen lemonade in a pitcher, he wandered around her living room, peering at the prints on the walls and titles on the bookshelves. He stopped for a long moment before a corner shelf where she displayed her favorite pieces of Pueblo pottery.

They sat at a table before the sliding glass doors, first downing a glass at a gulp, then sipping the cold sweet drink. "Your house is like picture in magazine I see at library." He raised his arm in a sweeping gesture, encompassing the pottery, Navajo rugs and leather sofas. "You have the Southwest style, I think."

She nodded, pleased that he had noticed the effects of her painstaking efforts to create the living space she wanted. "A few years ago, I was finally able to afford to buy some pieces that I really like. Now, this truly feels like home."

They talked about their jobs and their pastimes. His activities were apparently limited to work, running and reading books from the library. She knew a little about his department from the five years she had worked for the Lab before starting her own business. However, the technical aspects of it prevented her from making any intelligent comments. He wanted to know how she got into consulting.

"I didn't plan to have a business working with law enforcement agencies," she said. "And I didn't plan to live in New Mexico. I just knew I wanted to be far from St. Louis, and this is where I ended up"

He draped the towel over a chair. "You worked at Lab, but you are not scientist? he asked.

"No, I was an office manager. A friend helped me get my first job here despite my lack of scientific credentials." She silently thanked the former lover who had pulled strings to get her the position.

Ivan mostly answered her questions, not talking a lot, but the silences were not strained. She was unable to judge if this was due to natural reticence or unfamiliarity with English. He ran for an hour every morning before work, getting started at first light so he could have time to shower and eat before 8 a.m. In a desire to become more familiar with the area, each day he chose a different path among the maze that wound through the canyons. She gleaned this much before he brought the conversation back to her.

"You did not want to remain near family?"

"No. I knew early on that I wanted a different kind of life. Both my parents were professors, very intellectual and erudite. Children were nonessential elements in their lives. I never understood why they had a second child."

"Ah, Amelie. You were lonely child." It was a statement not a question.

"Yes," she said. "I was left pretty much on my own."

"But, second child. You have brother or sister."

"Yes, a brother." she said again, the old catch rising in her throat. "But he died." She took a big swallow of lemonade, choked and spluttered, dribbling on her shirt and the table. She became very busy blotting the spill. Death had taken her older brother when she was 15, followed two years later by her parents. She still missed her brother.

Ivan watched intently, making no effort to assist her. When she was able to speak again, she asked about his family. He replied that they were in Russia and that he had been away for a long time. She studied him when he looked away, thinking he resembled the ballet dancer, Mikhail Barishnykov — sensual lips, cool blue eyes, well-muscled body. She didn't mention this, fearing to reveal her nearly total ignorance of all things Russian. Barishnykov was one of the few of his countrymen, or women, she could name.

At promptly 7:15, he rose and thanked her, shaking hands in her doorway. "Tomorrow is Friday," he said. "We eat together at noon? I like chile you have here. We have nothing like in Chernogolovka. I go to Chile Works."

Amelie laughed. "Of course. You've already found the best food in Los Alamos." They agreed to meet at the local burrito stand and take their lunch to the pond in the center of town.

That morning Amelie called Lena and learned that Rusty had been arrested for theft. Carlton had told Walter, who had told Lena, that Rusty was also a prime suspect in Maria's murder. Some of the jewelry they found in his stash had been stolen from the Bath House, including a necklace with a large crystal that Serafina said she had seen Maria wearing.

Amelie recalled the defiant young man snarling at the deputies. Casting her mind back further, she tried to picture him slipping into the women's side of the Bath House and drowning Maria. The image wouldn't gel. He would have had to take off some chains or his clanking would have alerted every woman soaking in her cubicle.

Before hanging up, Lena had said, "Stop flirting with the Lab guys and get to work on my project. You told me you'd have something last month." She knows me far too well, Amelie thought, reviewing the morning's encounter.

She turned her attention to the papers she had collected on Jemez history, feeling once again the tug of procrastination that had delayed this job too long. Give her a computer and access to a database, and she could find just about anything. Reading old papers in small print and archaic language was tedious; it made her eyes hurt. Somehow when she had committed to this, she hadn't thought through the implications of researching property records back to the 18th century. Not too much on computer in those days.

She had learned that the Cañon de San Diego land grant had been awarded in 1798. More than 100,000 acres in the beautiful valley became the common holdings of a group of settlers. The twenty-five acres the Krazy Kokopelli sat on had to have been part of that grant, which had stretched from the existing Jemez Pueblo north to what was now Hwy. 126. Old land grants still appeared on many New Mexico maps. So far, she hadn't found any documents that showed individual ownership. Maybe she would drop this line of attack and work back from the present. Somehow, she had thought delving into ancient history would be more interesting.

Idly, she riffled through the file, thinking of Ivan and his tight shorts. Her hand stopped at the copy of an old photo which she had come across in a history of Sandoval County. Two rows of men in stiff white collars, black coats and trousers had posed under a huge cottonwood tree. Nearly identical pairs of black eyes under slicked-back black hair stared solemnly at the camera. She imagined them lining up at a nearby pump to wet their hair and wipe the dust from their jackets before posing for the photo. One anomaly caught her eye. A tall man in the back row was distinguished by blonde hair and light eyes. She squinted to read the blurry caption, and his name stood out as obviously as had his Nordic features. Amid the list of Hispanic names —Sandoval, Archuleta, Trujillo, Alvarado, Montoya, de Silva, Garcia —was Swenson.

Amelie looked hard at the unsmiling face of the Swedish settler. She'd heard the rumor that Maria Swenson's family had property here. This must be her —what? Great-grandfather? Great-great grandfather? She'd have to find the book again and check the dates. This wasn't aiding her much in Lena's project, but she couldn't resist digging a bit into Maria's family, although it was unlikely that it would have anything to do with her murder. Carlton's comments had erased any credibility Amelie might have put in Serafina's stories.

The mysterious Swenson was still on her mind the next day when she met Ivan, and they drove in her car to the pond to sit in the sun, eat burritos and drink iced tea. She wore a floppy straw hat and yellow sun dress. A line of light skin around the spaghetti straps showed the tan line of a tank top, her normal casual wear. Ivan was in what she took to be his regular work clothes: khaki pants and a plaid, short-sleeved shirt.

Amelie had brought a blanket, and they settled themselves on the grass. She told Ivan about her research into the old land grant. He was such an intent listener that she found herself relating the horror of that dripping body on the Bath House floor. She recounted the events surrounding the murder, unfolding the story in classic style, introducing the players one by one — Maria, the dreamy, spacey Spanish/Swedish victim; eerie Serafina, who'd found the body; Sage, the volatile boyfriend; Rusty, the unkempt boy with his tattoos; Carlton, the marshal with little experience in serious crime. Amelie went on to talk about her friendship with Lena and how, through her visits to the Krazy Kokopelli, she had come to know so many people in the Jemez.

"I just heard that Rusty was arrested," she said, concluding her monologue. "He had stolen things from houses and businesses all over the valley, including the Bath House. They may charge him with her murder."

"But you do not think he is killer," he commented after she had described what she knew of Rusty's arrest.

"Well, I don't doubt he's a thief and a generally disgusting character, but no, somehow that doesn't sit right with me."

"Sit right?" Ivan queried.

"Ah, never mind. My intuition tells me that's too simple, too pat, no, not pat. Too simple."

"Yes. I understand why you say that," he said, balling the foil wrapping of one burrito in a tight wad and unwrapping the end of his second. "What did you not tell me about your friend, Lena? I see in your eyes, in your hands, that something is not right in that telling."

Amelie stopped chewing, stunned. How had he picked up on that? Of course, she hadn't told him, or anyone, about Lena's long-ago, very brief, affair with Maria, nor her connection to Jenny.

"I, um, wow, you are a surprise. I'm amazed that you saw that." KGB, she thought. Aren't they all gone now? Ah, but, where did they go? "But you're right. She told me something that I can't reveal. Not to anyone."

"So, she has some prior knowledge of this Maria?"

Again, Amelie was startled into momentary silence. Did this man read her mind?

"As I just said, I can't tell you anything. I promised. Let's change the subject."

"As you wish," he said rather sternly. "You know, if there is secret about Lena and Maria, then Lena also is on list of suspects. You did not name her in your recounting. How high on the list depends on how much the secret."

Amelie, now convinced he was a police officer or spy in his former —or present —life, felt her heart pound faster. Why hadn't she seen that? She was intent on keeping the secret to protect Lena's relationship with her husband and her reputation in the community. And she always kept her promises. Never had she thought of her friend as a potential murder suspect. Now, as his words sunk in, that was all she could think of.

She needed to think this through. Lena, kill Maria? No, of course not. Gathering up the remains of her lunch, she told Ivan she had an appointment in fifteen minutes, not for a second thinking he believed her. They drove back to the Chile Works in silence, her mind churning with new possibilities. Not the least of which was the thought that Ivan Karnovich was a dangerous man.

CHAPTER 10

On a Friday two days later, Amelie was back at the Krazy Kokopelli. Lena had one guest that weekend, a woman from Natchez, Mississippi, who was writing her fourth novel. Amelie hadn't seen her, and Lena said the woman's routine was to come out for breakfast and then remain in her room all day, presumably writing. Every evening the mystery lady went to the Dancing Lizard Cafe for dinner, returned after dark, and ended the day with a long soak in the hot tub on the patio. Lena was usually in bed before her guest came in for the night.

Amelie had helped Lena put the finishing touches on the other three rooms, listening to her implore the goddess to send more guests. Slow weekends like this always put Lena into a frenzy of anxiety — she wouldn't be able to make mortgage payments, or replace the couch that was wearing out, or buy enough oatmeal to make her famous granola, or — the list of imminent catastrophes was endless.

Amelie hated to contribute to this downward spiral of doom, but she was finally ready to make the first report on her research into the history of Lena's land. In her briefcase was a list of the original settlers. Amelie also had checked on more recent real estate transactions, and there she had found some bad news for Lena.

Lena had purchased the deteriorating old adobe house and surrounding land in 1992. The sellers, Don and Eleanor Ramirez, and their agent both had assured her it was the original *casa*, that the house should be an historic landmark. Lena had intended to pursue getting listed on the registry as soon as she had the information that Amelie was gathering.

Unfortunately, Amelie had discovered that the 18th century structure had burned to the ground in 1920. A smaller house had been built on the site of the original dwelling, added onto over the years in typical New Mexico fashion. This was the house which Lena and Walter had converted to a bed-and-breakfast. While there was no question that she had a lovely, old territorial-style home, it was not one that had played a role in the early days of the Cañon de San Diego. Amelie had broken the news to Lena while they were drinking coffee on the patio, the gurgling of the river providing a backdrop to the conversation.

"Damn," exclaimed Lena. "I wanted to mount one of those plaques by my front door that said "Built in 17 — something." I could charge at least

$20 more a night for the privilege of sleeping where the conquistadors slept."

"They weren't exactly the conquistadors," replied Amelie. "They were farmers, which doesn't mean they weren't courageous. Think of coming all the way out here to this strange land with nothing but a few tools and your bare hands. I'm lucky to get sunflowers to grow! What a job to cultivate this land. Did you know the first settlement folded because they couldn't withstand the constant attacks by Navajos?"

"Navajos? Way over here?" Lena looked incredulous. "Yeah, I guess you're right. The rez starts just over the mountains."

"And the Navajo were raiders, not stay-at-homes like the Pueblo folks."

"Really. Maybe I could work that into my next brochure. 'Sleep where the brave settlers defended themselves from brutal Indians attacks.' "

"Oh, yeah. Great idea. Why not make it, 'Sleep above the bloodstained floor where wild savages scalped and raped the household.' Forget all this cute Kokopelli stuff. You could put a wooden Indian by the front door and hang some tomahawks on the wall. Most Americans think that represents all Indians."

Lena poured more coffee and sighed. "I wish I'd never asked you to look into this. Now I'll have to lie to have a historic B&B."

"Let your conscience be your guide."

Walter strolled onto the patio, empty cup in hand, and refilled it from the always-ready coffee pot. "Just saw Carlton."

Lena laughed. "I'm so surprised. You have coffee with him at the bakery every morning."

Walter ignored this. "He says they are definitely going to charge that kid with the murder. Serafina reported that she saw him and his girlfriend near the back door of the Bath House just before it happened. That's on top of finding a necklace that Maria always wore in the bag of stolen goods."

Amelie said, "Is Carlton supposed to be telling you this stuff? What if you're a part of the gang?"

Walter tamped tobacco in his pipe. "We're all a part of the gang." He struck a match and held the tiny flame at arm's length. "I warned the desperado that a posse was coming after him, and he's on his way to Mexico on his fastest horse." He lit the pipe.

"Walter," Lena cried. "Amelie just told me the worst news about the house."

"Dry rot? Termites? Roof leaking again?"

"It's only 70 years old."

"Then why should it leak? Isn't it a 100-year roof?"

"No, it's not the original house. That one burned. This one was built in 1925. I thought that was the year the plumbing was replaced. Now I learn this is original 75-year-old plumbing."

Walter laughed. "That explains . . ." and was interrupted by the sound of the front door opening. A voice said, "Anybody home?"

Walter called out, "Hey, Sage. What are you doing back here?"

"Hoping for a room for the night."

Amelie hadn't seen Sage since the hysterical scene in the marshal's office. Carlton had told Walter, who had told Amelie and Lena, that after the county investigation, Sage had been cleared of any suspicion in Maria's death. Apparently, Carlton still thought the man was guilty of *something*, maybe abusing Maria. Walter, who had been running into Sage for years at various gallery openings around the country, had dismissed this as Carlton's thwarted desire to arrest somebody and get the whole thing behind him.

Sage approached Amelie and grabbed her in a rough hug. "You know, I'm glad you're here. I never said thank you for trying to help me. I was in a real bad place that day. Really bad, man."

He kept an arm around her neck, pulling her against his body. Amelie had to push against him to extricate herself and took a step back. She felt revulsion toward the man that seemed deeper than the usual reticence about being handled by someone she barely knew. "You're welcome," she responded coolly. "How are you doing now?"

"Oh, you know. Good days, bad days." After casting her a sly look that said, I know I made you uncomfortable, he flopped down on the lounge chair where Amelie had been and turned to Walter.

"Harold Toya and I are doing a two-man show in New York next spring. Came down to work on that with him. He's amazing, man. Have you seen his sculpture?"

The two men talked artists and galleries, and Amelie drifted into the kitchen where Lena was opening two beers for the men.

"Lena, that guy gives me the creeps," she whispered.

Lena paused with a bottle in each hand. "I know. He's a little—no, a lot—stuck on himself, which always puts me off." She put the bottles on a tray along with a bowl of nuts. "Walter likes him, though. Not best friends like he and Carlton, but they talk about which galleries screw you the worst and the next hot place to show. They like to play poor artist."

"Well, I think I'll take a walk and read for a while. Is he going to stay here?"

"Don't worry. I'll give him the room at the end of the hall. Farthest from yours."

Amelie returned to her room and exchanged sandals for light weight hiking boots. She hopped from boulder to boulder to cross the river and hiked up a rough trail to the mesa top. After half an hour of unrelenting climbing, she reached a small plateau that provided enough flat space for a tiny meadow. The grass was dry and brown where she had counted eight kinds of wildflowers in the spring. At the north end was a pile of stones, the remains of an ancient field house. She came across these on every mesa top. She poked the toe of her boot into the dirt and uncovered a pot sherd, large enough to reveal a delicate design painted in black. Lowering herself carefully to avoid the ever-present prickly pear cactus, she lay on her back, watching a few white clouds drift across the azure sky. Her eyes closed. When she awoke, the sun had moved further west, and she was stiff from dozing on the ground.

Back on the trail, she noticed someone fishing in the river, standing knee deep in the water, casting toward a pool under a cottonwood. Glancing from time to time at the figure as she walked, she soon discerned it was a woman. Crossing at the same spot, she walked upstream to see what luck this angler was having today.

The woman scowled as Amelie approached, a clear "keep back" signal, then turned her back and cast again. Amelie hesitated then continued. This was part of Lena's land. The uninvited woman was the intruder.

When Amelie was thirty paces away, the woman turned again and threw her rod down on the bank as though her day had just been completely ruined. It was then that Amelie identified her. Jenny. Big belt buckle, cowboy hat, it had to be. The sturdy body in tight jeans was lithe and hard, but the face looked much older, darkened and lined. Furrows drew down the corners of her mouth and creased her forehead. A picture of pain, Amelie thought.

"Hi, Jenny. What are you doing here?"

The lines deepened even more, as she glowered at Amelie. "Whatever I want. Who are you anyway?"

"I'm a good friend of Lena's. I know who you are and what you've done. I want you to leave her alone. She has a great life here, a good business, a nice husband. You stay away. In fact, you're trespassing on her property, and I'm sure she didn't invite you. Why don't you just move on down the river."

Braced for a verbal if not physical fight, Amelie stood her ground and waited. Jenny attempted a laugh. "So, you're her protector. What's the matter? Her new husband can't take care of her?" She slammed her tackle box shut. "I need to talk to Lena, and not you or anyone else can stop me. Don't even try!" She stalked away along the angler's path and in a minute was out of sight around a bend.

Amelie sat down on a boulder at the river's edge, watching the now-empty trail, wondering whether to tell Lena about this encounter. Based on all she knew of Jenny, it was a relatively mild reaction. Her demeanor and language reminded Amelie of a thirteen-year-old. Dear God! What had ever made Lena give that woman a second glance? Pondering her next course of action, she finally realized that, short of sitting here all night guarding the path, she had no way of keeping Jenny from coming back. By the time she returned to the B&B, she had decided to keep quiet about the whole episode. Since her friend refused to enlist any help, there wasn't much else to do.

Lena was leaning on the kitchen counter in conversation with Serafina, whom Amelie hadn't seen since their meeting on the mesa. Four flats of strawberries spread a luscious banquet before them. One of the flats had been pushed aside, and Lena and Serafina were bent over the old photo Amelie had copied, the one where she had identified Maria's ancestor.

Amelie perched on one of the high stools and helped herself to a berry. "What's this?"

Both Lena and Serafina started speaking.

"Serafina picked up these berries for me at the Farmer's Market in Bernalillo. Aren't they beauties?"

Serafina tapped the photo with a fingernail and said, "This is my great-grandfather, Manuelo de Silva. He came here in 1798, one of the *primeros pobladores*. They were the first to work the land. Oh, how he worked, until he was 95 and dropped dead in the fields. The stories . . ." Her voice trailed off, and she looked through the high windows as though she could see out there the stooped man behind his one-horse wooden plow

Amelie hunched over to see the photo. "Show me which one is your great-grandfather, Serafina?"

The woman pointed to a figure in the front row, posed as stiffly as the others, face a bit blurred as though he'd turned his head just as the camera clicked. Amelie turned the copy over and wrote on the back: "Manuelo de Silva, 3rd from left, front row."

"Do you know who any of these others are, Serafina?"

"They were my great-grandfather's so-called friends," she said in a voice edged with bitterness. "First they helped him, then they cheated him and his family. Cheated me!" Her voice rose and she suddenly slammed her closed fist down on the photo. "Cheated me and my children."

Amelie and Lena exchanged glances. Amelie ventured first. "How did they do that? What happened?"

Serafina, breathing raggedly, had unclenched her fist and was staring at the long-dead men in the photo. "Some say it is witchcraft. Maybe so. I don't know. Witches, judges, lawyers, the Anglos, then our own friends. All against us."

She straightened and arranged her features into a tight smile, reverting to her gentle Bath House tone. "Enjoy your jam-making, Lena. I'll be sweating over a stove tonight, filling jars with sweet strawberries."

"Thanks so much for bringing these, Serafina. I don't plan to do much sweating though. Maybe a few jars of refrigerator jam, then freeze the rest." Lena gave the smaller woman a quick hug and walked with her to the door. "Thanks again."

She returned to the kitchen. "Wow. She's a little intense, isn't she? That's her way. She's very serious." She pushed one of the flats toward Amelie. "Here, earn your keep. We've got lots of strawberries to get through."

Amelie paused before picking up the little pincers that pulled the stems out. "Lena, she's got her dates all mixed up. The first settlers came before cameras. That can't be her great-grandfather. It's more likely that his great-grandfather was one of the, what did she call them, *primeros pobladores*. Amazing that she can get so worked up about something that happened so long ago. She really takes it personally." Lena was deep into her work and nodded absently, no doubt sending messages into the universe that she hoped would be answered by more travelers needing a bed.

The two women didn't leave the kitchen until the flats were empty. They had filled four pint jars with translucent red refrigerator preserves, which Lena would serve to her guests on homemade bread and biscuits. The remaining berries, washed and stemmed, were in freezer bags, waiting to be added to smoothies or made into jam later. By 11 pm, they were tired, stained with red on fingertips and lips, and more than ready to consume their reward: big, whole strawberries that they dipped in brown sugar and sour cream.

Amelie stretched her arms overhead, then massaged her lower back. Saying good night to Lena, she walked onto the patio, the sound of crickets filling her ears. The low hum of the hot tub motor cycling on and off mingled with the gurgle of the river. She thought briefly of taking a soak but decided instead to lie back on a lounge chair and look at the stars. Inside, the lights went out one by one as Lena moved through the kitchen and living room on her way out the other door to her little house. Finally, only one small lamp lit the silent inn. Sage had apparently left while Amelie was facing off with Jenny.

Amelie felt the dark closing around her, wrapping her in a private world. To her the shadowy night was comforting. She felt her smallness in the universe as she gazed into the black, star-studded sky, following the arc of the Milky Way. A rustle in the tamarisk by the river caught her attention. Raccoons probably, maybe a coyote or a stray dog nosing through the night, unseen in the black shadows.

She thought of all the secrets, hidden inside herself and others like the cover of night concealed the contours of the land. Lena was trying desperately to stuff her past into a hole and never let it emerge, pulling Amelie into a conspiracy of silence. Jenny, it seemed, was a one-woman vigilante posse, appearing where she was least expected, determined to elicit something from Lena. Serafina lived in some fantasy landscape that had been dead for decades, if not centuries, obsessing on fantasies of betrayal. The tattooed boy was locked away, out of sight, held in a jail cell for murder, his motives a mystery. Sage swung from charming to calculating; he faced catastrophe with heart-wrenching anguish alternating with cold detachment.

The bushes rustled and swayed again as a light breeze passed over her. Night creatures were on the move, and she was going to bed. She slipped through the sliding door and locked it behind her, determined to have peaceful dreams with no secrets haunting her.

CHAPTER 11

Serafina stood deep in the shadows of a towering cottonwood by the river, watching the back of the Krazy Kokopelli. At midnight, the moonless night was as dark as it was going to get. Only starlight illuminated the rambling house that was now a bed-and-breakfast. The glow of a small lamp colored the blank expanse of the sitting room windows. She could barely see the privacy fence surrounding the hot tub at the far end of the patio. Her cat-like eyes had adjusted to the darkness, and she saw outlines of furniture and the barbecue grill. While she watched, Amelie came out of the house and dropped onto the chaise lounge, becoming motionless. Serafina assumed she had fallen asleep, and she moved out from under the canopy of cottonwoods. She had replaced her habitual garb with black pants and sweatshirt and easily slipped through the tamarisk and low oak. She crouched and resumed her watching, waiting for a chance to approach closer, to leave her little memento, to make her mark.

This wasn't the first time Serafina had used her gift. She made potions and charms in the way her Tia Guadalupe had showed her. The people in the valley had feared her grandmother's sister; they said she was crazy. Yes, even her children and grandchildren, Serafina's cousins, had said the old lady was a *bruja* who could make people sick, cause their cows to die or their gardens to wither. What amazed Serafina was that these same people had come to Tia Guadalupe for help. Women mostly, silly women who wanted to injure a rival for their man's affection or make that man love no other.

Serafina had no use for love charms for those *chicas*, but she could make her enemies suffer. Lena had no idea that she, Serafina, was responsible for ridding the valley of the property's previous owners. The cancer that had tortured and finally killed that stupid woman with her Indian jewelry, Serafina had caused that. Now she would do the same to Lena. If a curse did not work, then she would use other methods, which she also had done before.

She had planned it all the day before. Then, after making jam at her sister's, she had started toward home, driving slowly along the unlit highway, alert for deer or cows on the road. Passing the Krazy Kokopelli—just the name made her want to scream—she had parked at the fishing access down the road. These little parks were sited at intervals along the river, another intrusion designed to attract more outsiders. She had walked along an anglers' path worn into the weeds at river's edge until she was back to Lena's property, then had taken a hidden vantage point in the darkness.

She remained immobile, her mind churning with perpetual outrage over the injustice she and her family had suffered. Lena had bought her property from one of the modern thieves, as Serafina called them. The bed-and-breakfast stood on land that was rightfully Serafina's. This afternoon in the kitchen, Lena had shown no remorse, not even the slightest sign that she was aware of her crime.

A movement on the patio caused Serafina to stiffen. Amelie sat up on the lounge chair and bent over, her head disappearing into dark shadow. Then she stood with something, probably shoes, in her hand, moved through the door and disappeared.

Serafina waited a few more minutes, then crept closer, feeling her way with her feet as much as her eyes, inching each foot in front of the other to avoid stumbling over cobbles on the path. In her hand was a crude doll, formed of the red valley mud into which she had blended long strands of Lena's hair, stolen on a previous visit from a hairbrush in the bathroom. Serafina had systematically pierced the soft molded figure with *aguja*, needles, then strangled it with thread until the head had been nearly severed. She had left it to dry in her special place, a place where she felt the most powerful. Now the time had come again to take her revenge. She didn't have to leave the doll near her victim for the curse to work, but she liked the idea of terrorizing those who knew what it meant. Maybe Lena would know, maybe not.

A new sound rose over the burbling of the river, a footfall. Then another. She slid sideways and pressed against the trunk of a giant cottonwood, holding her breath. The soft thud, thud continued without pause, and Serafina expected a deer to pass by, waited for it to bolt at her scent. Instead, a human shape emerged from the scrub oak and stood in a clearing, facing the Krazy Kokopelli. Dim starlight outlined a cowboy hat and glinted off a huge belt buckle. Serafina narrowed her eyes in an effort to see the face. The figure raised its arm and blinked a flashlight once, twice. Then the arm dropped, and the form waited without looking around.

Serafina became part of the tree, her breath shallow, consciously relaxing her hands which had tightened into fists. She was too close to the unknown person to back away; she had no choice but to wait and watch. From the building up the slope came the sound of a door opening and closing. She heard footsteps coming along the dirt path to the river. A voice she recognized as Lena's whispered through the darkness. "For God's sake, put that flashlight away. Someone will see us."

Another woman's voice answered. "Everyone is asleep. This valley goes to bed at 9 o'clock."

Lena footsteps seemed to have stopped several feet away. Serafina pictured how the land dropped away. Lena would be standing on a flat space that represented a long-ago river bank. Her voice fell to a husky tone. "I'm here, Jenny. What more do you want with me?"

Serafina felt like her ears were stretching, curving around the tree trunk and spreading to hear more.

"I told you in my poem. I love you. I'll always love you. I want to be able to talk to you."

Now Lena's voice sounded as though she were falling into a tunnel. "Jenny, what are you thinking? I'm married. Does 'married' mean anything to you? Our relationship is over—long over. I don't want to talk to you. I don't want to see you."

"I've changed, Lena. I won't hurt you."

"No, you won't. I won't let you. Please go away."

Serafina heard a quick intake of breath. A sudden sharp sound of boot on stone rang out above the river's ripple and the crickets' whine. "Lena, why won't you forgive me? Please. I'm trying to make up." Then the voice changed from pleading to belligerent. "Besides, I have a job. I'm here to stay. You better get used to it."

Lena sighed more deeply. "Jenny, go away. I agreed to meet you here, in the night, in secret, because I want — I hoped —" Her voice faltered, then faded as though she had turned her head away. "There's no point to this. Good bye." Serafina heard footsteps retreating up the path toward the bed-and-breakfast.

A second set of footsteps followed, tentatively, then faster. Serafina peeked around the tree in time to see Lena disappear into the shadows near the hot tub. The woman she had called Jenny stopped at the edge of the patio, then continued after Lena, the cowboy hat gliding in the moonlight until the gloom swallowed it up.

Serafina stepped from her hiding place and gingerly stretched her cramped arms and legs. She scrutinized the passage the two women had followed, ready to retreat if one or the other returned. She heard nothing more. She tried to imagine where they had gone. Obviously, Lena wasn't going to call for help. Serafina savored that fact. Lena was a disgusting *pervertida*. Somehow, sometime she would find that information useful. She crouched again, prepared to wait until she was sure it was safe to go onto the patio. The animal and insect sounds became loud in her ears. She let herself go into the dark sky, not feeling her weight on the ground. When she focused again on her surroundings, the stars had moved. Now, she thought, now I can do it.

As soon as that thought took form, a masculine shape moved like a *fantasma* across the patio toward the dark corner where Jenny and Lena had disappeared. Serafina at first felt like screaming with frustration, but then a small feline smile pulled up the corners of her mouth. Yes, they were blocking her plan, but maybe that was okay. This was like watching a play, seeing secrets played out on a dimly lit stage. Serafina heard the low hum of a motor and realized it was the hot tub circulating. Recalling the layout of the patio and the doors, she watched with fascination now, waiting for the next character to enter stage right. It was like some black hole pulled people to that corner by the hot tub and swallowed them.

Another hour passed, and she felt tired and distracted, no longer able to retreat into the trance-like state that allowed her to remain unmoving for extended periods. This was not going to be the night to complete her task. She would have to try again at another time.

She returned to the little riverside park along the path she had followed hours ago. Her feet struck the asphalt of the parking lot, and she knew she was almost to her car. Suddenly, an engine roared and bright lights flooded the area, holding her paralyzed for an instant. She quickly stepped back until she was safely hidden in a thicket, praying that no one had seen her. When her breath calmed, she peered around the corner, trying to see if someone was searching for her. Then a station wagon blasted off not ten feet away, tires screeching, gears winding. In an instant, the vehicle with its unknown driver was nothing but two red tail lights receding down the highway. She was left alone in the renewed quiet amid an odor of exhaust and burned rubber.

Slowly, she approached her car, her eyes searching the bushes in case an assailant lurked in the shadows. She unlocked the door and slid behind the wheel, reeling with fear —and questions. Obviously, she was not the only one spying in the dark. Why had the station wagon parked there? Was the driver one of those she had watched, or was someone watching her?

CHAPTER 12

Amelie awoke in confusion and bolted upright at the sound of a woman screaming and screaming without pause. She reached for a robe, unable to get her bearings. Sunlight streamed through the blinds of the east window. It was morning. She opened the door and ran down the hall, following the sound of what she now recognized as Lena's howls, interrupted by choked sobs. Hearing footsteps, Amelie looked back. Sage was close behind, surging down the hallway to the living room.

Bursting through the open sliding doors, Amelie reached the enclosure where the hot tub was ensconced on its little throne. Lena was standing at the open gate, her hands on her cheeks in the classic pose of horror. Lena reached for her, but Amelie pushed past her and went closer to the tub.

The woman's head had fallen back over the rim. Tangled, wet hair drooped down to leave a puddle on the deck. Her face was bloated and dark, the tongue protruding slightly. Her nude body floated in the water stirred by the jets, arms and legs rising and falling with the motion of the water. Amelie put two fingers on the swollen neck, seeking a pulse which she knew she wouldn't find. Drawing her hand back, she saw a pink line drawn around the neck as though it had been cut, connected to a similar line that ran down to each of the bobbing breasts.

Lena pulled her around, hands shaking. "What's wrong with her? Is she dead? Can you get her out of there?"

Walter appeared, put his arms around Lena from behind and pulled her away, murmuring into her ear. Amelie was face-to-face with Sage, a face that registered no emotion. My God, how awful for him, she thought.

"Dead," he said. "I'll pull her out." He took two long steps, grabbed the woman's arms and yanked.

Amelie clamped her hands on Sage's thick wrists, trying to release his grip. In doing so, she touched the slippery skin of the dead woman, still warm because of the hot water, but lacking the resilience that meant blood pulsing through veins. "Let go," she shouted. "Don't move her. We have to call the police."

"Oh, the police," he said in a flat voice. "I forgot." He released his grip and the body slipped back in the tub, submerged briefly under the water, then bobbed again to the surface, hair floating out like winter's brown weeds.

She looked at him, fighting to get her breath, prepared to give him solace.

Instead, she found him looking at her breasts, revealed when the robe opened as she had tussled first with Lena, then with him.

"Go call 911," she ordered.

Sage looked again at the floating corpse, sunlight glittering off the shiny skin, tiny waves still bouncing off the sides of the spa. "Okay," he said, still in that peculiar empty voice, and strolled inside as nonchalantly as though they had been discussing the weather. He must be in shock, Amelie thought. This has to be a horrible reminder of Maria's death.

She wanted to run away, escape this scene, so reminiscent of that afternoon in the Bath House. She stayed because she didn't want to leave Sage with the defenseless dead woman. He was practically leering at her in this tragic moment, and thinking that he might ogle the naked corpse made her gorge rise. She would keep vigil with this woman whom she'd never met. A natural inclination to cover the body was stalled by the knowledge that doing so would disturb the scene even more. Carlton's comment about moving anything at a crime scene echoed in her ears.

Amelie slumped to the deck and leaned against the fence, her body angled so the hideous scene was out of her line of vision. Slowly, the rising sun and the sound of the river calmed her, although the presence of the body was like a burning hand on her back. She could dimly hear Lena sobbing inside the house and Walter's soothing voice talking through the crying.

The image of a pink line on the dead woman's neck and chest appeared in her mind, side by side with the image of Maria's neck, a similar line cut into the flesh, ensnaring a gold chain. Two women strangled and drowned in hot tubs. The sanctuary of the Krazy Kokopelli violated. She shuddered.

The sound of a car turning into the drive meant Carlton had arrived. Another murder for Carlton. She hadn't spoken with him since their lunch at the bar. The door to the patio slid open. She rose and turned slowly.

He stood there, one hand on the gate, eyes scoping the scene. They came to rest on her, as she stood with arms hanging like lead weights at her sides. Then, unintentionally, incongruously, she was aware of a quickening inside, an alert of body and heart. He looked tired and anxious and totally appealing. She had an urge to put her arms around him, to feel his strong, warm embrace.

Carlton took a step, and she thought he would reach out to her, but he stopped as though checking himself and turned to look at the body. She gestured toward the hot tub and its horrible contents.

"I checked her pulse. Useless, of course. No point in doing CPR," Amelie said.

"Did you move her?" Carlton was at the edge of the spa now, leaning for a closer look at the distorted face and injured neck. Then he walked around the hot tub slowly, scrutinizing the decking.

"I didn't move her, but Sage did. He started to pull her out." Amelie hadn't stirred from the spot where she stood when he entered. She kept her eyes up toward the trees, the sky, anyplace but the hot tub. Carlton's sharp voice made her jump.

"Dammit, Amelie. Why did you let him do that?"

"Why? Dammit yourself, Carlton, he didn't ask permission. I stopped him as fast as I could."

As though she hadn't answered, he continued. "And what are you doing here again? Waiting to see me make a fool of myself a second time?"

She started to reply, but he cut her off. "Don't say anything. I don't want any advice."

He lifted his cap to run a hand through his hair. She waited, thinking he would calm down, tell her he was sorry that she had to witness this, but his mouth remained set in a grim line. "Another murder scene contaminated," he growled. "Just my luck."

Amelie couldn't hold back any longer. "Just your luck?" She flung a hand blindly toward the spa. "I'd say she's the one with the bad luck today."

At that he looked at her. Again, she thought he would soften and come to her, or at least apologize. Instead, he asked, "Do you know who this is?"

"I assume she's staying here, but I didn't meet her. Lena mentioned a guest who liked to get into the hot tub late at night."

He nodded, and then resumed his search, moving in wider and wider circles toward the privacy fence. Just then the motor started again, automatically turning on the jets to circulate the water, and they both jumped at the sudden sound. The body began to float in a circle, moved by the motion of the water.

"Christ," moaned Carlton. "How do you turn this thing off?"

"The controls are right there. Turn the knob with the arrow down to zero." Amelie dreaded to get closer and was relieved when the abrupt cessation of sound told her he'd found the dial. She pulled the robe tighter around her. "I guess I'll go get dressed. You don't need me here, do you?"

"No, you go on." He was walking along the fence, still searching the decking.

She paused with her hand on the gate and turned back to find his eyes following her, the expression unreadable. "Another one, Carlton. What in the world is happening here?"

CHAPTER 13

Very late that night, Amelie let herself into her apartment. She kicked off her shoes and sank into the sofa, too tired to start her bedtime ritual, which was brief anyway – brush hair and teeth, wash face, apply moisturizer. During the forty-five minute drive back to Los Alamos, she had gone over and over in her mind the events of the day. First, Carlton's unreasonable anger toward her, then the endless wait for the sheriff's deputies to take her statement, and through it all Lena's devastation. Not only was her friend horrified by the death, but she soon began to agonize over the effect this event would have on her business. Who would come for a relaxing weekend getaway to a place where people got murdered in the hot tub? That this was a murder, there was no doubt. Amelie had seen immediately that the strangulation and mutilation of the body was not an accident, and Carlton and the deputies had referred to it as murder without waiting for a medical examiner's report.

Carlton had remained distant, polite and inscrutable. Not a word of sympathy, barely an acknowledgment that they were acquainted, although he had been earnestly compassionate with Lena. She had replayed this as she sped along the forest-lined highway and navigated the curves past Bandelier National Monument and down the mountain. Yes, she had told him they could no longer be lovers, but she thought they could remain friends. He was acting like a child. Friends help and comfort each other during bad times; he and she had a history. The more she thought about it, the madder she got.

Friends acted like she and Lena. The two women had sat with their arms around each other, alternately crying and commiserating, making endless pots of coffee and giving themselves permission to snack on the truffles Lena put on guests' pillows. While Walter was being questioned in the small first floor guest room, Amelie had again begged Lena to tell the sheriff about Jenny. Lena was adamant. Even mentioning it had resulted in renewed sobbing. Once more she made Amelie swear to never, never tell anyone about that old relationship.

Amelie's eyes jerked open as her body started to tip toward the pillows at the end of the sofa. Wearily, she pushed to her feet and padded to the bedroom. Dropping her clothes on the floor, she fell into bed and slept like a stone.

She awoke to a pounding on the door. She swung her legs off the bed, straightened stiffly, and pulled the curtains aside an inch to view the front porch. Ivan stood there in his skimpy shorts and tank top, jogging in place. She slipped into her robe and went to the door, pulling it wide as she ruffled her hair into place with her hands.

"Hi, Ivan," she croaked, her voice husky with sleep.

Ivan looked at his watch. "I am surprise you sleep too late. You want to run for me on beautiful morning?"

Amelie looked around at the sun-blessed ponderosas like she was surprised they were still there.

"Ah, yes, it's beautiful, but I had a really hard day yesterday – and it's Sunday morning – and – do you want to come in?"

He appraised her costume. "Yes, I come in, but I prefer run before the breakfast."

"A run will do me good. Please sit down. I'll get dressed and have a quick glass of orange juice." She turned and started for the bedroom, but he put a light hand on her arm.

"What is 'hard day'?"

She slumped against the wall. "Another murder. This one at my friend Lena's bed-and-breakfast." She held up a hand before he could speak. "I know she's your chief suspect, but she couldn't do this."

Again his hand was on her arm, guiding her toward a chair next to the table. He pulled another chair opposite, and they sat with their knees touching, his hands on her shoulders.

With that touch, she lost the composure she had held so tightly yesterday, being strong for Lena, being tough for Carlton, eschewing the behavior of a hysterical woman who would fit the deputies' stereotypes. Silently, tears streamed down her cheeks, her shoulders shook and finally, she caught her breath in one big sob and let herself cry. Ivan gathered her onto his lap and held her like a child, murmuring Russian words into her ear and stroking her hair. The phone rang, but she ignored it.

Finally, she wiped her eyes and nose on the sleeve of her robe. "I don't know how to help Lena. This isn't something that happens to me regularly, you know. I can't get the pictures of those dead women out of my mind. The minute I woke up, there they were."

Ivan continued to pet her, now stroking her arms and back. Then he nuzzled his face into her neck. "Poor little goat. You don't want to be detective."

"No, I don't. I want to do my job and visit my friends and get in a hot tub without thinking about being strangled." She choked, and the tears started again.

"Yes. Yes, you do." Ivan was kissing her neck, and she suddenly was aware of his body, of her nakedness under the robe, of the fact that for once he wasn't paying much attention to what she was saying. In fact, she had lost interest in it herself. She put her arms around his neck, feeling the hard muscles of his arms tighten around her. He held her close to him for a moment, and then one hand moved inside the loose robe and caressed her breasts, fingering the nipples.

When he moved his mouth toward hers, she put a finger on his lips. "I'd like to continue this, but I feel like . . . I feel like I just got up. I need a shower, okay?" Without waiting for an answer, she slipped off his lap and went into the bathroom. When she came out, a box of condoms in hand, he was lying naked on her bed.

She threw herself on top of him and, for the next hour, was lost in the familiar rapture of sex, seeking the release that obliterated every thought and image in her head. He was a skillful and surprisingly playful lover, delighted to discover the tattoo on her breast and the matching one on her hipbone, where his lips returned again and again. He laughed like a happy child at the shrieks her orgasm produced. Only once, when he was moving his mouth down her body for a second round, did she unexpectedly see Carlton's face, hovering above her.

"No," she said aloud to the specter.

Ivan lifted his head. "No?"

"No, I mean . . . Not, no. Just ignore me. No, don't ignore me. Just do what you're doing." She squeezed her eyes shut tight and let ripples of pleasure erase the image.

Both were dozing in the patch of sunlight coming through the window, when Amelie was awakened by the phone ringing. She had no intention of answering and was annoyed when the caller didn't leave a message. After they dressed, she fixed scrambled eggs and toast for breakfast. Across the table, she told him the details of the second murder. Immediately, he attacked the problem.

"Where was Lena last night?"

She groaned. "At her house, in bed, I assume. I don't know. You can't think she'd murder someone on her own patio!"

He ignored this. "Who else was there?"

"Walter, of course. Definitely not the homicidal type. He went out to his studio right after dinner. Sage Hansen, the boyfriend of the first woman who was murdered. I think he's kind of a creepy guy, but I know the sheriff's office checked him out, and he was cleared of any involvement in Maria's death. Me, and the murdered woman, that's all."

"No others?"

"A woman from the Bath House dropped by earlier that afternoon, and I ran into . . ." she stopped herself, ". . . another old friend. Those are the people that I know about." She remembered his uncanny deduction about Lena's secret, and his next words proved that their recent intimacy had not dulled his incisive ability to read her unspoken thoughts.

"I know you want to keep secret. To protect friend, I think." He paused, waiting for a response. She looked out the window, fingers tapping the rim of her coffee cup.

"When I see secret, I have suspicion. Will you not tell me? Perhaps I help you."

Amelie rose to pour more coffee. With her back to him, she replied, "I can't tell a secret I don't have." She could feel his speculating gaze on the back of her neck. After a moment's silence, he surprised her by asking again if she'd like to go for a run. Apparently, he was not going to press her to reveal anything more.

Amelie had no energy for further physical activity. She declined and, after he left with a chaste kiss on her cheek, sat again at the table to finish her coffee. Although she had dismissed Ivan's queries and offer of help, whatever that might mean, she was in turmoil over her promise to Lena. Jenny, volatile and violent, might well be involved in this. She was surely on the scene earlier, skulking around Lena's property. Jenny had been involved with Maria, conceivably could have become angry enough to kill her, but Amelie couldn't imagine that she also had a connection to the second victim. She considered that Jenny might have killed this woman to get back at Lena by ruining her business, but that seemed really farfetched.

The problem boggled her mind, and she longed to talk it over with someone she could really trust. And that person, she knew, would be Carlton. She had to tell him. He could act as though he'd discovered Jenny's activities on his own and reported to the sheriff. Lena would never have to know that Amelie broke her promise. At least not until they laughed about it twenty years from now.

She felt the relief of having made a decision. With renewed energy, she cleared the dishes from the table, turned on the "Golden Oldies" radio station, and danced toward her office. Maybe she couldn't help Lena deflect the horror of the coming publicity, not to mention the suspicion of various law enforcement agencies, but she could continue her work on the land history project. Also, the thought crossed her mind that work would still the voice inside that said she had just done a really stupid thing. Again she had used sex as a sedative, a substitute for other feelings, a way to avoid thinking about anything unpleasant.

Her recognition of this pattern had come a few years ago, when she had been camping at Wild Rivers Recreation Area near Questa and day-hiking into the Rio Grande gorge. The weekend trip was an attempt to get over being dumped by a judge in Magdalena. On her second morning there, she had awakened in the back of a Volkswagen van next to a man she'd met the previous day on a hike. She had looked at him in chagrin, crept from the camper, and walked the quarter-mile back to her own campsite. There she sat in an aluminum lawn chair for the rest of the day, oblivious to the incredible view, only seeing herself on a merry-go-round of one man after another – always having fun, always enjoying the sex. Almost always.

Settling into her office chair, she recalled that she had driven from Questa to Lena's. They had sat in, yes, her hot tub for an hour. Lena told Amelie she had long been worried about this pattern. Amelie reviewed a few heated conversations in which Lena had asked what she was doing with that loser, her term for whoever was the current boyfriend. Amelie had been defensive each time, always responding by saying, you just don't know him. Now, she was starting the ride again. Sex with Ivan was fun, but who was he to her? This was recreation not a relationship. Confection. Straightening her shoulders, she reached for a notepad. She'd think more about this tonight.

The second bedroom in the apartment had been transformed into an office. Shelves lined one wall, filing cabinets another. Against a third wall was a desk, computer and work table. She pulled the land grant files from a drawer and spread them in front of her. Several weeks ago, in a spurt of energy, she had obtained a list of the original settlers from the state archives in Santa Fe. Then she had gone to the Sandoval County Courthouse in Bernalillo and looked up records of transactions on the land where the KK now stood. Until today, she hadn't taken time to pour over the blurry, hard-to-read old copies, some in Spanish.

Now she methodically followed the paper trail of deeds and sales and court rulings. Lena bought her property from Don and Eleanor Ramirez, who had moved from Santa Fe. They had held the land only three years, after purchasing it from the San Diego Land Company, Christian Swenson, president. The land company had purchased 44,000 acres in 1926 from Harold

Swenson, a lawyer by profession, according to the letterhead. Amelie remembered feeling the embossed print when she had copied the yellowed letter. Prior to that, the land had been part of a grant made in 1798 to a group of colonists as was common at that time.

Amelie sat back and tapped her pen on the edge of the table. The original land grant had covered the whole of Cañon de San Diego, much more than 44,000 acres. A huge portion of the grant had been lost by 1926, and she wondered where it had gone. Just curiosity. She didn't need to know that to give Lena the history of her land that was emerging from the records. The other thing that piqued her interest was Swenson, apparently a Swede. She remembered the tall blonde man in the photo amid dark-eyed, dark-haired Hispanic pioneers and wondered how that pale Scandinavian had come to be in the Jemez.

She flipped through more papers and found a decision in which the Land Claims Court, in 1859, had awarded land to a list of Hispanic settlers. The names were those prevalent in the valley today: Garcia, Gonzalez, Lopez, Gallegos, Apodaca, Jaramillo, de Silva. She would bet these were the same families who had been awarded the huge tract by the Spanish crown.

She reviewed the list of *primeros pobladores*. Swenson, obviously, had not been among them. But he had been awarded at least a half-dozen claims in 1859. She skimmed the names on the deeds she had copied. Over the years, Christian Swenson had bought parcels from a number of buyers. Again, she recognized several names as being those of people she had met in Jemez Springs. One of those names was de Silva. Serafina was a de Silva, but hundreds of families in New Mexico shared the old surnames.

The room had grown darker, and she stood to stretch, reaching her arms to the door jamb and arching her back. She hadn't dressed all day, a habit she often had when working at home, and the robe fell open as she swung her arms overhead to loosen her neck.

The doorbell startled her, and she peeked through the blinds for the second time that day – and for the second time saw a man on her doorstep. Carlton. Synchronicity. She had decided to tell him Lena's secret, and within a few hours, he appears.

Suddenly she felt like "I've just had sex with another man" was written across her forehead. She yelled, "Just a minute," and raced to the bedroom to throw on sweat pants and tee shirt. She scrubbed her hand across her forehead and opened the door. His fist, apparently raised to reinforce the ringing with knocking, stopped two inches from her nose.

"Hey, Carlton, I know you're mad, but don't hit me."

He looked at his hand like he hadn't put it there. "Hi, Amelie. Can I come in? How are you?"

She bit back the impulse to scold him for not asking that when they were at the KK. "Fine. I slept, then I worked. Kept my mind off that poor woman." She turned into the living room. "Come in and sit down. What did the deputies say?"

"Gave me hell for walking around the patio, disturbing another murder scene. I can't do anything right as far as they're concerned. They're not too happy with anyone, it seems. A Sandoval County judge released Samuel Arthur Cooke, aka Rusty, yesterday, after his rich daddy's lawyer came through with bail. So their – our – prime suspect was out and about last night."

"Serafina's dirty boy? Out of jail?" Amelie threw her hands up. "Well, why don't they arrest him again?"

Carlton was seated opposite her in an old rocking chair that had been her grandmother's, an anomaly in the room furnished with two sumptuous leather sofas. He dropped his hat on the heavy glass-topped coffee table. "They're looking. I'm supposed to be looking, too, but I wanted to see you, so I looked all along Highway 4, and somehow ended up here." He leaned forward to rest his elbows on his knees. "I wanted to be sure you were okay. I tried to call a couple of times, but you didn't answer. I didn't leave a message because I wanted to apologize in person. I feel bad that I wasn't very nice to you this morning."

This was what she had wanted, waited for him to say. If he'd come at 8 o'clock this morning, she would have welcomed him with open arms. Now, she was finding it hard to keep this conversation going. "Sure, I'm fine, or as fine as I can be after seeing a second murdered woman. Want a beer or some coffee?"

He opted for a beer, and she went into the kitchen to get two bottles out of the fridge. Carlton excused himself and walked down the hall to the bathroom. When he returned to stand beside her at the kitchen counter, the atmosphere had changed. She could feel it; the air sizzled.

"Stuck my head in your bedroom to turn off the light. Wish I hadn't looked. Then I wouldn't have seen, known what you've been doing."

Amelie fiddled with the glasses she had set on the counter. "Seen what?" And then she knew. The half-empty box of condoms lay on the bedside table. She hadn't put them away. The bedroom probably reeked of sex.

"Come off it, Amelie. I'm not the stupid country boy you think I am. I'm a trained law enforcement officer, remember. I observe. I collect clues. I was just a little slow on this one, until it hit me in the face." He shook his head. "The way you looked at me this morning at the KK. I thought if I came here, and we talked, we could work this out."

She kept her head down, looking at the fake wood grain pattern in the Formica. "I didn't know you'd come here today, but I was glad you did. You were just the person I wanted to see." She picked up a beer and started to pour it into a glass, her eyes blurring with tears. Thoughts blurted out in an adolescent rush. "I'm so tired of trying to figure this out. Why can't I love a nice man like you, and settle down, and be happy? Why am I doing this?"

She heard the words as though from someone else and considered them. Doing what? She needed an answer but first had to define the question. She had been in therapy, knew that she lacked trust in others, especially men. Even an armchair psychologist could connect that to her parents' affectionless and distant behavior throughout her childhood. Then, her beloved brother had died and left her to her own devices. Finally, a drunken driver had killed both parents, destroying any possibility that she would ever feel any love from them. But she thought she had "worked through" all that, thought she was an adult free spirit. who wanted to be independent. The old familiar thoughts raced around in her head like a whirlpool in a riptide.

She kept the bottle tilted and tried to pour into the glass. Carlton took it from her as liquid spilled off the counter top onto the floor. She waited for him to shout at her, expecting the angry words she deserved. Instead, he gently set the bottle down and took her hand to lead her into the living room. He pushed her onto the sofa and sat beside her, still holding her hand.

"I don't know the answer to your questions, Amelie." When she glanced up in surprise, his sober brown eyes were searching her face. "I wanted us to have a traditional, simple, faithful relationship where we loved only each other. I don't pretend to understand why you aren't interested in that."

He carefully put her hand on her thigh and turned away to rumple his hands through his hair. "I do know this. You think I'm a hick cop, stuck in a little village, who doesn't know much about the big world out there. But I've seen a lot of different people in a lot of different circumstances. I know a runner when I see one. You're hiding from something – something in yourself. I don't have to be a rocket scientist to see that." He scooped up the Baca cap and pulled it low over his eyes. "I have no idea why."

Amelie stared at the door that closed behind him. Found out in every way.

When did he get to be so smart and she so dumb? She blushed to think about how supercilious she had been toward him. Good, old, simple Carlton. God!

She sat without moving until she was stiff and cold. The scene repeated in her mind, and she felt ashamed every time she heard his words. Finally, she walked to the kitchen and poured the beers down the sink, then wiped up the mess on the floor. She realized she really might never see him again, that she had lost the illusion of control she once believed she had in the relationship. She feared that he had given up, and the thought was desolating even though this was what she had thought she wanted.

While going through the motions of washing dishes, her mind leaped to escape depressing thoughts and settled on the previous problem. She had decided to tell Carlton about Jenny, and now the opportunity was gone. What next? Anonymous letter? Mystery call to the sheriff's office? She moved back into her office but was unable to lose herself in the maze of land transactions. She dropped her head onto arms crossed atop a pile of files.

She wanted to keep her promise to Lena, return to Carlton's good graces, enjoy the excitement of Ivan's touch, and, she realized with some surprise, honor two dead women by helping to find their killer. All seemed mutually exclusive and hopelessly difficult. She had no standing with the sheriff's office and certainly had lost all rapport with Carlton. Her pledge to Lena prevented her from revealing the person who she believed was the most likely suspect. She resolutely refused to consider Ivan's suggestion of Lena's involvement. Amelie Jameson, girl detective. What a joke!

CHAPTER 14

Lena sat in the shade of a cottonwood on the deck at Deb's Deli, gazing absently in the direction of the road. Puffs of dust billowed as each vehicle passed. The water was low in the acequia that ran between the restaurant and the road, and she noted the debris of modern society—mostly aluminum cans and plastic bags—that floated in the historic irrigation ditch. An occasional breeze lifted the edges of the napkins under the silverware and swept strands of hair back from her face.

She was meeting Amelie for lunch at noon, but she had left the KK at 11:15, fed up with the babbling of an elderly couple from Indiana who couldn't seem to figure out how to spend their time. They had sat on the stools at the breakfast bar long after she had cleared the dishes and poured their umpteenth cup of coffee, asking details about every attraction in the area. Would they get too hot walking around State Monument? Were there picnic tables at the Gilman tunnels? How much time should they allow to visit the Soda Dam? Was the Friday night prime rib really good at the Rio Jemez Bar and Grill? Would she like to join them that night for dinner? At that, Lena fled, calling her lunch date with Amelie a business meeting for fear that they would invite themselves along.

Now she waved at friends who walked past and chatted with those who paused at her table, but her mind was ranging in the past, remembering her month-long affair with Maria and her year-long relationship with Jenny. She had left Oklahoma at 17, dropping out of high school in her senior year with the promise to herself and her grandmother that she would get a GED. Instead she had gotten pregnant, had an abortion, and went with her 25 year-old boyfriend to Seattle. They were drunk and high most of the time, holding odd jobs until they lost them, buying as much beer and weed as they could afford, staying in a tiny house in Tukwila through days she couldn't remember. Then one night he never came home, and she never heard from him again. Her new boyfriend sold drugs, weed mostly, but he took whatever came along, plus he liked liquor, and sex. He was her man; she did whatever he asked and took whatever he offered to anesthetize herself. They partied in all combinations: men and women, women and women, men and men, couples, trios or all together. And Maria had come to some of the parties. Maria, who never looked jaded, who fucked everyone out of "love," and more than once was there holding Lena's hand when she came to. Maria

Swenson, a Swedish-Hispanic girl from New Mexico, who said she came to visit her uncle in the Scandinavian neighborhood of Ballard to get hydrated, to smooth the sun-dried wrinkles out of her flawless skin.

The drug dealer got busted, Lena had nowhere to go, and Maria invited her to move into her apartment. Maria explained carefully that they were put in each other's lives for a special purpose, to learn from each other, then to move on to the next lesson. Lena got a job tending bar at The Wild Rose on Capitol Hill, a mainstay of Seattle's lesbian scene. She reasoned that she was sleeping with a woman, so she must be a lesbian. Then Maria found her new lesson, a Jamaican man who played in a steel drum band, and Lena was homeless again. That's when she met Jenny.

Trying to remember why she had thought she loved Maria, she realized their frenetic life was mostly obscured by a continual drug and alcohol fog. Jenny drank a lot of beer, but refused all recreational drugs, even marijuana. She told Lena a person couldn't be an alcoholic if they drank only beer. Lena was 19 and already had been dumped by two men and one woman in the two years since she'd left home. Jenny had seemed a pillar of stability with her regular job, no-drugs policy, and paid-up, clean apartment. Lena accepted Jenny's frequent fits of temper. After all, she was a fuck-up and she knew it. But one morning Jenny really lost it. Apparently she thought she could pound attraction to males out of Lena.

When Lena woke up in the hospital, she knew something had to change. She cleaned out their joint bank account, took a bus to the airport, and literally got on the next flight with an available seat, which turned out to be to Albuquerque, New Mexico. The path to her GED, to being drug-free, to owning her own business, to getting married had been tortuous. But she had made it. She was safe here. Or she had been.

Adrift in her memories, Lena was startled when she heard her name, recalled to the present by a woman who owned another bed-and-breakfast in the valley. They talked shop for a while, but in the background hummed the refrain that was always there. She would never talk to me if she knew what I've done. I could never live here if anyone knew. They couldn't even imagine the life I've had.

"Hey, girlfriend." Amelie arrived, hugged Lena and greeted the other woman who left after a few minutes of small talk. They ordered, and Amelie looked intently at Lena.

"What's wrong?"

"What do you mean, what's wrong?" Lena feigned surprise but gave it up when she saw the knowing look on Amelie's face. "I was just thinking about Maria, about Jenny, about the other person I was then. Thinking how quickly life can turn and kick you in the butt." She gave a rueful laugh then her face hardened. "I'm not giving up what I have here, Am. I mean it! I'd do anything, anything to keep the hounds at bay. I feel them nipping at my heels, trying to pull me down and destroy me."

Amelie gripped her friend's trembling hand. "I know you're worried, but try to relax. I wish I could say something reassuring. Unfortunately, there's not much you can do right now." Amelie paused as a teenage waitress set down their lunches. Lena asked the girl if she'd passed her calculus test and listened patiently to a long description of how hard it was.

Amelie took a bite of her grilled chicken and green chile sandwich then asked, "What's the latest on the hot tub victim?"

"Her husband came from Mississippi to identify the body. Can you imagine how horrible that must be?" Lena felt tears form and blinked to keep them back. "Carlton and the sheriff's deputies searched the deck, every room in the house, and the land for a mile around. Lots of tracks by the river, of course, but nothing that represented a clue. You know that after they questioned you, they questioned Sage, who said he was asleep in his room, and Walter who was out in his studio, designing a new glass piece. A detective came back yesterday and asked me the same questions again. Did I hear or see anything? Did she seem afraid? Who knew where the hot tub was? About a million people, of course." She wiped at her eyes. "According to Carlton, they can't uncover a motive for her murder. So far, they can't find a link between her and Maria."

"What about the boy with the tattoos, their suspect for Maria's murder?" Amelie asked.

"Now that's interesting. Someone came in to tell Carlton they saw an old station wagon that night parked at the fishing access south of the KK. Apparently, it looked like Rusty's, but they haven't found him yet. Maybe he's gone up into the mountains."

Amelie asked the question Lena had been dreading. "Does anyone know where Jenny was?"

"Only me."

"What?" Amelie choked on her sandwich. Grabbing a napkin to stifle her cough, she looked like she was going to jump up and shake Lena.

"You can't tell. You promised. Remember?" Lena felt her lifeline extended only to Amelie. "Just listen. Don't yell at me. She called and wanted to see me. I met her by the river, just for a couple of minutes, then I went home, and so did she, I guess."

"You guess?" Amelie had recovered but still looked astonished.

"She started to follow me, then I didn't hear her any more. I didn't turn around. I told her I wasn't going to see her again, and I meant it."

"Lena, could anyone have seen you and Jenny?"

She shook her head emphatically. "We were near the river, which makes it hard to hear voices. It was totally dark, and I didn't see anyone."

"And you shared this with the deputies, or with Carlton?"

The edge of sarcasm almost put Lena into a panic. "Of course not. Are you crazy? Do I have to tell you again that I will never, never reveal this secret to anyone but you?" Her mouth burned with the intensity of her words. She had to trust someone. This was her best friend. If Amelie didn't stand by her, then she was alone. "You have to stick with me here, or I'll crack up."

"I know. I will. I just wish you would let Walter help you, too." For every time that Lena had railed at Amelie for what she euphemistically termed her fooling around, Amelie had nagged Lena to trust Walter with the story of her past. More than once, she had been close to confessing to her husband, and confession was what she imagined it would have to be. If she told him the truth, she would have to beg, on her knees, for absolution for deceiving him into thinking she was someone else. She had rehearsed the speech time and again, but the words never came.

Amelie again reached for her hand, then squeezed and withdrew as a shadow fell across the table.

Serafina walked by in her customary black garb, holding a styrofoam take-out box in her hand. Lena forced herself to sound untroubled and casual. "Why don't you join us?"

Serafina declined the invitation. "I always take my lunch and eat by the river. I can be alone there."

Amelie patted the adjacent chair and also invited Serafina to sit down. "I've been looking into the history of Lena's land. I think I mentioned that the other day. Maybe you can help me with my research. Turns out Christian Swenson got a lot of land in the late 1800s. Did your grandfather or anyone in your family ever talk about that? I'd like to understand how it came about."

Lena's mind was still in turmoil, and she barely registered the turn to discussing land history. She noted, however, that Serafina stiffened at Amelie's questions, and her fingers had tightened on the to-go box.

"I told you my grandfather was cheated. I don't wish to discuss it further." Her voice rose. "My family has taken care of ourselves for years. We will continue to do so." Without saying goodbye, she descended the steps and marched across the parking lot toward the Bath House.

Lena made an attempt at their normal banter. "You certainly know how to rile her up. She'll be a great source of information now!"

Amelie had recoiled at the strong reaction from Serafina, but shrugged in response to Lena's jibe. "Yes, I cultivate my informants with the utmost care." She finished the last of her iced tea. "Something is really off with that woman, Lena. I'm not sure what it is, but I think she has some kind of personality disorder. Seriously. Maybe you've had normal conversations with her, but every time I've talked to her, she has been weird. That's my professional psychiatric diagnosis as a software consultant."

They walked across the road to where Amelie had parked in the bar's lot. They stood in the hot sun while Lena, at Amelie's request, repeated word-for-word her exchange with Jenny on the night of the second murder. Amelie reciprocated by telling Lena about her last conversation with Carlton.

Lena felt her mouth squeeze into a prim circle, and she observed with slight amusement that this was an issue that could distract her from her present state of self-pity. Feeling like a prude, she admonished Amelie. "What are you doing, going to bed with an Ivan? Amelie, I thought you were going to keep your panties on and wait for Mr. Right, who, in my opinion, is Carlton, although you've probably ruined that relationship forever."

For a minute she thought Amelie would flare up in self-defense, and they would have another argument on this subject. She could see a fire building in the other woman's eyes, but it died, and Amelie relented. "You're right. I've blown it with Carlton. I know anything with Ivan is just for fun, which –" She held up a stop sign hand. "–which I'm not totally against, even if you are. But I thought, at my age, I could handle all this a little more gracefully. Instead, I'm alienating people I care about, including you, and disappointing myself." She leaned back against her car. "Do you think Carlton will get over it?"

"Not over this." Lena didn't hesitate. Through Carlton's friendship with Walter she had come to know the marshal fairly well. Her mind digressed into the thought that Carlton above all would hate her if he knew of her irresponsible past. She continued, "He takes every relationship very seriously. He never plays the field, never cheats on the woman he's with – and he hasn't been with that many. This is a knife to his heart, Am. You pushed it in and twisted."

Amelie groaned. "That makes me feel so much better, dear friend. I just –

I know, silly me – just wanted us to be friends. I feel like I should apologize, but I doubt he'd listen." She twisted her bracelets idly then stopped abruptly. "You know, this is going to sound really, really silly, very Miss Marple, but I think I can help him solve this murder. For one thing, I can . . ." She stopped.

"Can do what?" Lena asked.

"Never mind. Just thinking. I'll let you know when I have the usual suspects assembled in the parlor." She laughed to herself as she imagined playing the role of the clever elderly lady in Agatha Christie's fiction who solved murders in her small village.

Lena glanced up as the marshal's car pulled to a stop in front. "Well, don't look now, but your former paramour just arrived. And he's in a hurry. Must be trouble in the bar."

Amelie made a show of squinting at her watch as though she didn't know it was mid-day. "Little early for the drunks to get rowdy, isn't it?"

"A little but not unheard of. Keeps Carlton on his toes. He and his deputies would get fat and lazy without this place."

Amelie straightened up and turned, and it occurred to Lena that her friend had been steeling herself for a confrontation with Carlton. Not that he would make a scene in public. He would tip his hat and act like he always did, serious and polite, a well-brought-up boy.

They both gaped as a woman's voice roared, "Let me go, pig!"

Amelie lifted her eyebrows. "Pig? When's the last time you heard that?"

Lena shushed her. "Look who he's got in custody. She's drunk. And angry, like always when she drinks."

They stared openly as Carlton gently but firmly pushed Jenny into the back seat of his patrol car. She wasn't handcuffed, but he looked like he wished she was when she started pounding on the inside of the door.

The marshal's car pulled away, engine sounds drowning out muffled shouting in which the words "brutality" and "pig" recurred frequently. Carlton looked neither right nor left as he drove the few hundred yards to the cop shop. Lena doubted that he had noticed her and Amelie.

"I sure hoped never to see that again." The slight relaxation of tension she had felt during their discussion of Amelie's peccadilloes had vanished at the sight of Jenny. She gave her friend another hug. "I have to go see if my pesky guests have found something to do so they'll be out of my way." Plunged again into the grip of anxiety about the murders, she shuffled to the other side of the parking lot. She prayed without much hope that Jenny would be sufficiently cowed by an arrest, if that's what it was, to leave the valley.

Fumbling in her purse for keys, Lena bumped into what she assumed was her white truck. It took a second to realize that the white pickup she was trying to fit her key into was not hers. With a second look, she saw the horns mounted on the hood and backed away. Jenny's truck was parked next to hers. Had Jenny planned to be there waiting when Lena returned to her vehicle? Sunlight flashed off an ornament hanging from the rear view mirror, and Lena gasped. She stepped forward again to see more clearly the design of the pendant hanging from a gold chain. A woman's head. Lena recognized the necklace. She'd seen it on Maria in Seattle all those years ago, and Amelie had said she had possibly seen it in the Bath House when Maria was killed.

She turned and ran back to where her friend was ready to exit onto the highway. "Amelie! Stop!"

The other woman braked and rolled down the window. "What is it?"

"Come here. I want to show you something!" Amelie looked like she was going to ask questions. "Come. Now!" Obediently, Amelie parked and followed.

They walked to the driver's side of Jenny's truck. "There." Lena pointed.

"Yes. It's Jenny's pickup. Who could miss it?"

"No there. On the mirror. It's Maria's necklace. She always wore it."

Amelie pressed against the truck door to get a good look at the ornament. "You're right." Amelie angled her head this way and that trying to get a clear view. "I think I might have seen her wearing one like that when I first met her, and it might have been with the others next to her tub, but I can't be sure."

"Did you see Jenny in there that day?" Lena rested her cheek against the truck window, staring at the necklace.

"No, but wait. Someone left who I thought was a man because of the cowboy hat. It could have been her. Hard to tell. Everything was so chaotic."

Lena stepped back and pulled on Amelie's arm. "Let's move away. We look ridiculous."

Amelie allowed herself to be dragged away from the cowgirl's truck. "This convinces me that Jenny was there when Maria died, but I still can't understand why she would kill the other woman, if that's what we're thinking. And I really don't know why she would display this necklace if it was Maria's. Is there anything else you haven't told me?"

Lena crossed her heart and strove for a light-hearted tone. "Nothing. I swear." She sorted through her keys again. "Now, I'm really going home to face the guests from hell. You can solve this mystery, can't you, Miss Marple?"

On the drive home, Lena thought about the implications of the necklace. Jenny must have been at the Bath House when the first murder occurred; Jenny had been outside of her house the night of the second murder. Jenny was driven by convoluted thought processes to separate the world into those who were for her and those who were against her. Lena knew Jenny succumbed to murderous rages. But no matter how she looked at it, Lena couldn't fit the latest victim into the picture.

The phone was ringing as she opened the door. "Krazy Kokopelli, how may I help you?" she chirped.

The voice that responded was Carlton's, speaking in a tone of utmost sorrow. "Lena, I hear you were acquainted with our first murder victim."

CHAPTER 15

Amelie pulled her standard business uniform from the closet and put it into a suit carrier. She had three sets of slacks and matching jackets – one tan, one navy blue, and one black – plus five silk shells in various pastel colors. Add an assortment of jewelry and scarves, and these could get her through a week, if necessary, but she would be in Hillsboro only one day. An advantage to this destination was its proximity to Truth or Consequences, where she planned to find a modest motel and have a nice long soak each morning and night at one of the many hot spring spas there. She would drive the 200 and some miles today, do the follow-up training tomorrow, and then drive back the following day.

Passing through her office to get the laptop, she paused before the stack of files on Lena's land history. The photo of the *primeros pobladores* threatened to slip from its folder, and she pulled it loose. The picture fascinated her. She felt like a message was hidden in the somber faces and rigid postures of the long-dead men. Giving in to curiosity, she pushed duty aside for an hour—that's all she'd give to this today, an hour.

Seating herself in the office chair, she propped the old photo against the base of the lamp and pulled the bulging folder toward her. Tucked in the back was a small book, which a look inside showed was way overdue at Mesa Public Library. She had marked the page where a discussion of the Cañon de San Diego grant started, intending to come back to it later. This was later. As she read, the story of what had happened to the land grant unfolded. A not-so-flattering picture of Christian Swenson emerged as well, a man who had not lived up to his name, who had practiced neither charity nor kindness toward his neighbors. I doubt that anyone with the name of Swenson was ever welcome in the valley, she thought. Even though it was all legal, the old families must grind their teeth when they drive through that land. Lena had no idea what shenanigans had resulted in her current ownership of the property.

Amelie allowed herself to be diverted by the thought of Lena, so distraught, so resolved to be the woman she had painstakingly molded herself into. She had seen Lena's determination before and, reviewing examples of the woman's tenacity, thought of Lena's trip to Ponca City, Oklahoma.

After she and Lena had been friends for several months, Amelie had learned another of Lena's secrets. The only positive legacy of Lena's alcoholic mother was her passion for fancy dancing. Amelie had once gone to the Gathering of Nations in Albuquerque, one of the largest pow-wows in the country, and watched in amazement as girls twirled around the arena in time to the drums, fringed shawls flying and moccasined feet barely touching the ground. Lena had once been one of those girls. Her mother had taught her daughter from the time she could walk and, as a young teen, she had competed in pow-wows all over the country—when her family members weren't too drunk to take her. She had resumed going to pow-wows when she came to New Mexico, although by that time she had left fancy dancing to younger women. Now she danced the traditional women's dances. Amelie had seen her at the Jemez Pueblo Powwow, moving in stately cadence to the drum beat, showing no resemblance to the jittery woman who straightened throw pillows every two minutes at home. Last year, when Lena had learned that an aunt she thought long dead was alive in Ponca City and that a pow-wow would be held there, she set herself to go in style. She had worked every night for two months to make a beautiful buckskin dress and taught herself beading, doing it over and over until she was satisfied that it was perfect. She was driven like a mad woman to present herself as a traditional Kiowa matron to her aged aunt. She was welcomed by this remnant of her family, and Amelie imagined that when the drums started and her friend's moccasins stepped onto the floor, no one would know she hadn't been there forever.

Amelie straightened in her chair. The hour she had allotted herself was up. She gathered her things to place by the front door, then turned abruptly, grabbed the folder and shoved it into her briefcase.

She mulled over the problem as she sped south on I-25. The modern interstate paralleled the historic *Camino Real*, the royal road that had once brought settlers, soldiers and priests along the Rio Grande from Zacatecas, Mexico, to Santa Fe, the capital of *Nuevo Mexico*. The bosque lining the Great River of the West was a bright green swath in a brown, barren land-scape. To the east and west rose small mountain ranges, companions of the Sangre de Cristo and Sandia Mountains that were the bulwarks behind Santa Fe and Albuquerque. She reached TorC at mid-day and decided to stay at the Riverbend, a funky set of cabins set right on the river. In twenty minutes, she was up to her neck in hot water, literally, choosing the hottest of the three square tubs set outside on the river bank. When her body temperature threatened to go over the top, she followed a short path through the willows and plunged into the swift current, holding onto a rope provided as tether. For 45 minutes, all thoughts of the murders, the settlers, of anyone or anything related to Cañon Springs were suppressed.

But the thoughts returned the next day, hovering in the back of her mind as she went through her standard spiel for the Hillboro sheriff, her deputy and clerk. Often they had to repeat their questions, as she stared out the window while they set up practice files. They were disgruntled by the end of the day, and she knew this had not been one of her finest hours. The following morning she was up early, foregoing a final dip in the hot springs, determined to get to the Albuquerque Public Library in time to look at old issues of the *Tribune*.

Twelve hours later she was driving with abandon up the steep incline of Hwy. 501 toward Los Alamos. She had never become inured to the stunning views of Pueblo Canyon, into the side of which the road had been blasted out in the 1940s. The floor of the canyon was lost in deep shadow this late in the day. Orange walls, pocked with black openings of all sizes, rose from sparse cover of piñon and juniper. Some of the holes had been enlarged centuries ago into small caves that had housed ancestral Puebloan people. Hanging on the canyon rim were modern habitation sites, ranch houses of the Atomic City's more affluent residents, windows sparkling in the setting sun.

Wearily, she turned onto Walnut Street, planning to call Lena the minute she got inside to tell her about the discovery at the library. Another part of her mind was planning the post-training report she would write tomorrow. Maybe a prompt, brilliantly comprehensive report would erase the poor impression she had left in Hillsboro.

Surprised to see a vehicle at her curb, she recognized Lena's truck as soon as she pulled up behind it. Since Lena rarely left the KK except on her shopping days into Albuquerque, Amelie knew this meant an emergency. She winced because she could guess what would cause this uncharacteristic behavior. Somehow Walter had learned of Lena's closely guarded secret.

She approached her friend's truck and was surprised when the figure behind the wheel didn't move. Amelie thought perhaps she was asleep, then her heart thudded at a worse possibility. Could Lena be tormented enough to be suicidal? She ran forward and yanked open the door. To her relief, Lena jerked up. Amelie's relief faded when she saw a gray, bleak face, eyes unfocused as though pulled from a trance

"Oh, Amelie. Carlton thinks I did it. Did it to protect my secret past. He called me in to his office. Giving me a break by talking to me before calling the county sheriff." The words spilled out like a dam had burst, like she could not have waited much longer for Amelie to arrive. "What was I saying last week? 'I'd do anything.' I should have qualified that. Anything but murder!"

Amelie helped Lena to the house. The other woman's limbs were lifeless, each step seemed to take great effort. Once through the door, she dropped like a stone onto the sofa, face set in the same zombie-like mask she had worn outside. Amelie started coffee, deciding it was no use speaking until she could jump-start Lena with some caffeine. In a few minutes, she was adding milk and sugar to Lena's cup. After she pushed it between her friend's limp fingers, she asked, "What happened? How did Carlton find out?"

Lena didn't move for a long minute. Then her hollow voice replied, "From Jenny."

"Dammit. She spilled the beans when Carlton took her to his office?"

"Yes. She apparently told him quite a story. He probably thinks that Walter is next on my hit list, so Jenny and I can get back together." She finally took a sip of the hot sweet liquid.

"Lena, give Carlton some credit. He knows that you and Walter love each other. Speaking of, what did Walter say?"

At that question, Lena seemed to shrink a few sizes. She put her cup on the coffee table and fell back into her trance.

"Lena?"

Finally, she spoke. "I don't know. I left a note and drove here. I didn't see him."

"Oh, Lena. You have to talk to him." Amelie put her arm around her friend's shoulders. "He loves you! He's not going to take this the way you think, but it would sure help if he hears it from you. And he's got to be frantic by now."

"Too late. I wrote that I'm leaving, that I can't do this to him."

Amelie got up to bring the coffee pot, then realized that Lena's cup was nearly full. The room had grown dark, and she turned on a lamp. Lena flinched at the light, cowering against the end of the sofa like a beaten animal.

Amelie sat in the rocker. "Has anyone proposed a motive for your crime spree?"

"Well, of course, it's obvious." Amelie was heartened when Lena roused enough to be sarcastic. "I killed Maria so she wouldn't tell about my past. Then I killed that poor woman from Mississippi because she heard me and Jenny outside by the river. Jenny apparently told Carlton about that, too. Anyway, the theory is that my guest was in the hot tub and overheard us arguing. When I discovered that she was there, I killed her to keep her quiet."

She held her hands out. "Lethal weapons. You should be afraid to be in the same room with me."

"Yeah, I'm scared shitless. Actually, I am, but not of your killer hands. I'm scared that you think you have to be a brave little martyr, all alone. This isn't like you. You should be calling a lawyer, yelling 'false arrest,' doing everything to fight these stupid charges." Amelie stood, waving her arms to emphasize her words. "Mostly, I'm scared that you're just letting your marriage go down the drain when you don't have to." She knelt and took Lena's hand. "Please, please call Walter. Let him help you. Nothing will hurt him more than being shut out right now."

Lena raised her head. "That's what you would do, not me. I'm too tired to fight."

Amelie scooted onto the sofa, hip to hip with her friend, and they sat in silence. Each tick of the grandmother clock in the hall resounded through the house like a death knell. Finally, she felt Lena's shoulders shake and knew that the tears had started.

Amelie heard the clock strike 8, then the chime for the half hour. She thought about fixing dinner and gave Lena a squeeze as a signal that she was going to move. Lena held on tighter, holding so hard that Amelie was aware as never before of her friend's fear. Amelie patted her back like she was soothing a baby and, in a voice croaking after the long silence, crooned, "There, there. Everything's going to be all right." Banal words without a shred of foundation, she thought. How are we going to get this straightened out? Her attempts at comforting words, were interrupted by the sound of a car stopping in front of the house. She went to the window and lifted a slat of the blinds. Ivan was coming up the walk.

"Damn! This is all we need now." He had come by her house twice in the past two weeks, sweating from his run, obviously expecting that they would repeat their sexual adventure. Both times she had put him off with some excuse or other. Never before had he visited in the evening, and she was puzzled. She opened the door and said, "Well. What a surprise!"

Ivan paused expectantly on the porch, waiting for Amelie to let him in. When she didn't do so, he opened the screen and held it aside with his body. "I am come to say I have sorrow for you and your friend."

Amelie was stunned, not for the first time, at his seeming ability to read minds. "How did you know?"

"It is on television news."

Relief that his ESP was illusory was quickly replaced by horror at this information. "Oh, no! I didn't even think of that." She stepped back, and he brushed past her into the foyer.

"They say they are searching. She is fugitive. I think she is here. I think that is her truck."

Amelie's first impulse was to deny that Lena was there and to get rid of Ivan, but something told her that would not be possible. His eyes gleamed, and his nose practically twitched, like a bloodhound on a trail.

"Yes, she's here. She didn't do it. She's scared and confused, and we're going to figure out what to do."

"I will talk to her."

"Ivan! She doesn't even know you."

"I will talk to her and learn truth," he replied and moved into the living room as though she had invited him in.

Amelie stepped around to block his path. "I know the truth. I've told you. She didn't do it."

Their raised voices brought Lena's head up. She looked in confusion from one to the other. Amelie relented. "Lena, this is Ivan. Ivan, Lena."

Amelie noted that as a measure of how deeply Lena was depressed that she didn't show a flicker of interest at the man's name. Just last week she had admonished Amelie to "never see that Russian guy again."

Ivan stepped forward to hold out his hand. "Pleased to meet you."

Lena's eyes darted to his face and down again. She didn't move or respond.

He acted like this was normal. "I will ask questions of you. You will answer. When I finish, we will know what happened."

During the next half-hour, Ivan impersonally and methodically questioned Lena. Interrogated might be a better word, Amelie thought. Many of his questions were the obvious ones: who, what, when, where, why. It was the why that Ivan focused on, and that included a lot of background. He extracted information in a short time that Lena had only revealed to Amelie over the course of years. He must be a professional, Amelie thought. He's done this many times before.

Having nothing to do but act as hostess, Amelie offered drinks. Ivan settled for water when he learned she had no vodka. Lena, to her friend's amazement, refused coffee or anything else. However, she couldn't help but notice that Lena's face had a little more color. Some shift had occurred as Ivan's soft, persistent voice pelted her with questions. His detachment appeared to have a grounding effect, and Lena answered willingly, without confusion, and without adding anything beyond the scope of his queries.

Amelie had heard the story before. She was barely listening, but a change in tone signaled he was finished. He thanked Lena and had turned to speak to Amelie when yet another knock summoned her to the door. She didn't bother to check but flung it open—and was face-to-face with Carlton in full uniform.

Without preamble he said, "Amelie, I know she's here. I have to take her in."

"Take her in? Carlton, don't be ridiculous. You can't do this." She actually stamped her foot. "Lena didn't murder anyone."

Carlton's dark eyes were troubled, and he didn't smile. She knew from the set of his shoulders that further argument would be futile. He was going to follow through with what he saw as his duty. He all but pushed her aside.

Stepping into the living room, he actually put his hand on the butt of his gun when he saw Ivan. Amelie assumed that reaction was surprise at finding anyone else in her living room and extreme anxiety at having to arrest his best friend's wife. She piped up like the perfect hostess, hoping to defuse the situation. "Carlton, this is a friend of mine, Ivan Karnovich. Ivan, Carlton Duran is marshal in Cañon Springs. I believe he's here to arrest Lena."

Ivan extended his hand. Carlton ignored it, and Amelie saw his fingers tighten on the gun.

When Ivan spoke, Amelie was amazed that his astonishing prescience had deserted him. Nothing he could have said was more likely to offend and anger the other man than the words that came out of his mouth. "Marshal Duran, I think I can help you. I learn from Lena—"

Carlton, jaw clenched so tight that Amelie thought his teeth would crack, interrupted. "I don't need any help. If you would just step into the hall, please." He gestured with his head and stepped aside a scant inch or two. His demeanor clearly showed that Ivan would be dispensed with before any further proceedings. The two men were frozen for a moment, each waiting for the other to move. Amelie had a flash of an Old West confrontation, *Reach fer yer iron, stranger.* If she hadn't needed to protect Lena, she would have turned and run out the back door.

Lena remained seated where she'd been for the past few hours, but she was closely attending to the drama, her eyes shifting from one to another as they spoke. Everyone turned in surprise when she rose, walked to Carlton, and held out her hands, apparently expecting to be handcuffed. "I'll go with you. Are you ready?"

Before he could respond, another loud knock startled them all. Amelie muttered about putting in a toll booth and turned to answer. Before she could reach the door, Walter burst into the room.

CHAPTER 16

Amelie's small living room was a whirlwind of emotion and movement. Lena shrank behind Carlton, as though she were trying to efface herself into invisibility, all the time looking anywhere but at her husband. She hissed at Carlton, "Get me out of here. Now!"

Walter pushed past Amelie toward his wife, only to confront Carlton, who shifted from foot-to-foot in agony, caught once more between feelings and duty. Amelie watched the tableau for an instant before thrusting herself between the two men and saw Carlton's perplexity change again into anger – mostly, she thought, at himself for being stuck in this dilemma. Walter gained momentum and growled, "Out of my way, Amelie. I'm not letting my wife get arrested by anyone, not even him."

Amelie stood her ground and was shocked to find herself being strong-armed aside by the normally placid Walter. He shoved hard enough that she stumbled back against the wall, reaching for a chair to keep from falling. From the corner of her eye, she saw Carlton jump to restrain Walter.

Suddenly, over the panting and thumping of their struggles came an authoritarian voice that stopped them all in mid-motion. "You will cease this. Without delay." Ivan followed this command with a string of equally terse orders in Russian. He hadn't shouted, only raised his voice a notch. No one could understand the words, but the intent was crystal clear.

Ivan stepped forward before they could catch a breath and resume the conflict. He addressed Walter first. "You are angry guy. I understand. But do not have worry. Your wife is not guilty. There will be formalities, but she will be freed. Please to step back." When Walter opened his mouth, ready to argue, Ivan preempted him. "You will not fight with law officer. Understand?"

Apparently confident of compliance, he turned his back on Walter to face Carlton, whose body blocked Lena, "You must do your duty, but I see your heart. You do not want to do this." He nodded toward Amelie as though they were long-time partners. "Amelie and I will fix. We will reveal truth."

Finally, he addressed Lena who cowered – Amelie had never thought she would use that word to describe her friend – in the corner. "You are foolish. You run away and act with guilt. You hide from husband. Maybe he forgives you." He shrugged, saying wordlessly that he wouldn't if she were his wife. Then, with a quelling look at Carlton, he said to Walter, "You have five minutes. Take her to other room." To Lena, he said, "Go!"

Looking dazed, Lena stepped forward and, still not meeting Walter's eyes, walked down the hall and disappeared into Amelie's bedroom. Walter followed and in the hush that ensued, the three in the living room heard mumbling, the gasp of a sob, then silence.

Amelie felt herself coming up for air. She needed to take control back from this foreign man, who so naturally assumed command of everyone right here in her own living room. "Ivan, thank you for defusing an explosive situation," she said formally, using the tone she reserved for recalcitrant members of a training group, the ones who always challenged her to prove she knew more than they did. "You seem quite sure Lena will be exonerated. Of course, so am I," she added. "In the meantime, what is it you think we know, and what are we going to do?"

Carlton spoke up. "Well, for starters, she's not under arrest. Not by me anyway, unless she resists. I'm pretty sure they don't have enough evidence for a charge, although she is acting guilty as hell. I'm going to take her to Bernalillo for questioning by the sheriff. And I wanted to find her before one of those deputies . . ." He broke off, looking at Amelie as though pleading for understanding. She stared at him without response. He continued, shaking his head in bafflement at Lena's behavior. "Unless she confesses, which she might given how she's acted today, she'll be home by morning." He lifted his ever-present cap and ruffled his hair in a gesture so familiar to Amelie that she found herself on the verge of a smile. Recalling the crisis facing them, she resumed her severe expression.

Carlton looked thoughtfully at Ivan, and Amelie could almost see him deciding how to play the next scene. He opted for conciliation. "Mr. Karnovich, is it?" Amelie was amazed that he could remember an unusual name in the midst of the chaos just receding. She was reminded that he often confounded her. Ivan nodded, and Carlton continued. "You seem to have some experience in these matters." He paused, leaving the hint of a question hanging in the air. Ivan didn't speak, and the pause lengthened. Carlton relented. "Okay. I'll just leave the two of you to work it out while I take my friends out of here."

He headed for the hallway, stopping to face Amelie, eyes scanning her face, searching for something from her but revealing nothing of himself. She felt her arms flex to lift to him, but he moved on and she let him pass. In a moment, she heard him knock on the bedroom door. "All right, you two. Let's go." Lena and Walter must have been waiting for a signal, because the door opened immediately and the three trooped out the front door without another word.

Amelie slumped onto the sofa, and Ivan took a seat next to her. They didn't touch or speak, and Amelie's thoughts raced over the events of the past hour, scene after scene replaying in her mind. Inevitably, she realized what she *should* have said, *should* have done.

Ivan broke the silence, speaking in a conversational tone. "When I talk to your friend, I see she is not killer. I have seen. I know. She is . . ." He waited for an English word that did not come. "She waits. She suffers. She does not fight, not try to stop the source of her suffering. She will take pain . . ." He put his fist over his heart. "She hold inside, and she wait. I do not know how to say better. I know she cannot kill someone to take away pain."

Amelie said peevishly, "I told you that already. The question is, how do we prove it?" She realized she had said "we," as though the two of them were going to work together. Unlikely, she thought. He has no real interest in Lena. I have to figure this out myself.

Ignoring her irritability, he continued. "You know because you want to believe. She is friend. This is what friends do. I know because I talk to her. She is not friend to me, but I have, ah, have curious?" He looked for confirmation of his word choice, and Amelie nodded without correcting him. "Yes, I have curious. I am scientist. I like problem to solve."

Amelie said, "Okay, I'll bite." The immediate consternation on his face would have been humorous in any other situation. She realized he must think she was diverting him with an invitation to more sex play. "Sorry, ignore that. Tell me what you think will clear Lena."

In the next half-hour, struggling to put his thoughts into coherent English, Ivan traced his reasoning. First, he said, his analysis of her personality was that she would not attempt to protect herself through murder. She had no history of violent reactions as evidenced by the fact that she had not retaliated against Jenny even when she had been abused in Seattle, nor when Jenny had appeared at her home in Cañon Springs and threatened her. Lena's overriding concern was to quell scandal by concealing her past, and in that context, she would avoid any rash action that would potentially call attention to herself. In addition, Maria appeared to have made several visits to the Valley during the past few years. If she had wanted to kill her, Lena would have had other, less public, opportunities.

However, these were speculations, not data that would stand up under the scrutiny of a court. He had elicited a number of interesting facts, however, all of which opened the possibility that others were equally suspect.

First, no one had come forward to say they saw Lena at the Rio Jemez Bath House—or even in the village—on the Fourth of July. Lena also had talked later with several women who worked at the Bath House, including Serafina, who was complaining as usual about newcomers, land-grabbers and thieves. As proof that she wasn't paranoid, Serafina had offered the information that some of Maria's jewelry had been stolen before the murder, again accusing the "dirty boy." Lena had told Ivan she had no way of knowing if Serafina, who distrusted everyone in authority, had shared this information with the police. Lena had also heard that the day before the murder Maria had told the clerk at the trading post, who had told Lena, that Maria was frightened because she had found an evil charm under her front step. Maria had refused to describe this spell because, she had said naming it gave it power, but she was convinced she was being targeted by a *bruja*. Maria had been heard to say she was ready to clean up her land, sell it for a lot of money, and take a trip to India. Neither Carlton nor any of the other authorities had been interested in all this gossip.

Finally, Ivan had questioned Lena closely about the night of the second murder and elicited new information. Lena, not volunteering anything to direct attention to herself, had not previously told anyone but Amelie about her late-night encounter with Jenny, nor that she had gotten up at 2 a.m., wandered into the B&B and seen that Sage's door was open. What she could not say for sure was whether Jenny had surreptitiously returned, or when Sage had come back from the bar. Finally, Walter had come looking for her, coaxing her back to bed. So, Ivan had concluded, everyone was moving about, which gave them all opportunity. The difference was that, in the eyes of the police, Lena had not only opportunity but motive.

At the end of his recital, Amelie was unconvinced. "There's nothing new here, Ivan, except that I didn't know until recently that she was out and about that night at the KK. I've told you before." She extended her hand and started counting off points finger by finger. "The police already cleared Sage. Carlton says Serafina's been nuts for years, and he discounts anything she says. Maria was well-known as a hippy-dippy person who milked every little thing that happened to her for maximum drama." She waved away his look of confusion, not stopping to interpret 'hippy-dippy' or 'milked' and rushed on. "I still think the best bets are this Rusty person, who is out on bail, and Jenny, whom I know to be violent and vengeful. I'm sure Lena told you we saw a necklace of Maria's in Jenny's truck, a necklace she must have stolen?"

She broke off, rose to her feet and gestured toward the door to usher him out. "I'm tired, too tired to think anymore. Tomorrow I'll go back to Cañon Springs and – " She didn't yet know what she would do there. Look for clues, she guessed, whatever that might mean.

Ivan held her back at the door. "I see also you have," he paused, "love with marshal. Makes more difficult problem."

She didn't attempt to deny this. "Yes, it does. Good night."

He left without further protest, but his knowing look told her she was going to hear more of his theories at a later date. She wasn't ready to accept his assumption of a partnership. She needed to get the story straight in her own mind, or— Tired as she was, an idea flashed into her head. Stories! These events represented more than one story. She was trying to fit it all together, and maybe that would never work, perhaps there was more than one puzzle to solve.

She was in bed within minutes, wriggling into the soft mattress with relief at being horizontal. Her brain seethed with the night's emotion-laden multiple encounters: Lena's collapse into depression and inertia, Walter's unexpected assertiveness, Carlton's confusion and ambivalence, Ivan's exposition of his deductions, her own inability to step up and take hold of the situation. She felt she was niggling at the edges of the problem, assembling factoids, little pieces of evidence, all the while missing a larger, overarching view. Was that what Ivan was seeing – the big picture? Waiting for her nerves to quiet enough to allow her to sleep, she thought about Ivan's report on his examination of Lena's motives. According to Lena, Maria had claimed that she was bewitched. In Amelie's research on the land history earlier that day – was it only that morning? – she had read anecdotes of settlers who claimed all their misfortunes – failed crops, stolen cattle, barren wives – were due to witches.

Thinking of the early landowners and their subsequent troubles brought to mind the ruin that Serafina claimed as home. She knew the history of that land now. One of her discoveries was that Serafina's family had been one of the big losers in the often nefarious land transactions taking place around the turn of the century. Theirs had been a large extended family. Brothers, uncles, and cousins together had owned numerous plots of irrigated land and had the largest cattle herd grazing the common land that had been part of the San Diego grant. While Amelie had not yet been able to pin down the exact boundaries of their irrigated holdings, she suspected it extended from the broken-down adobe Serafina had shown her from the mesa top north to Lena's land and beyond.

Tomorrow she would go back there and think it through on the ground. She would hate to have to tell Ivan he was right about anything, but somewhere in the stew made up of her research and his analysis was a key that she couldn't quite grasp. Too tired now, she thought. I'm sure when I'm not so beat I'll think of something that will exonerate Lena once and for all. I'll get it straight tomorrow.

CHAPTER 17

Rusty plodded along on the track to the ruined house, sweating and cursing as he stumbled in the ruts. He had, for once, let Ellie take the station wagon, figuring if the police were looking for him, they would follow that. He climbed over a fallen cottonwood that blocked the so-called road and splashed through puddles left in the red dirt by yesterday's afternoon thunder storm. Under one arm was a six-pack of beer and a bag of potato chips; under the other a ragged sleeping bag. Ellie would come back after dark with more food and beer.

He had spotted this old wreck of a house last week when they were just driving around. Sure, the sheriff had let him go, but who knows when they'd change their minds. They had enjoyed busting him. He'd slept sitting up last night, leaning against the crumbling walls. Tonight, he'd wrap up in this sleeping bag, which made him feel better because things had kept crawling on him, and he had to jump up every other minute and brush off whatever it was. He stopped before what was left of the front door. A lizard slipped across the fallen adobes and disappeared into the darkness inside. What a shit hole! This place had all kinds of bugs and spiders and—Fuck! He'd crap his pants if he found a snake in there.

He jumped as a hummingbird zoomed past his head. Fuck! Something was always crawling or flying all over the fuckin' place. And it was too quiet here. He needed some music! And the temperature must be a fuckin' 200 degrees. Now he couldn't remember why he ever thought leaving Albuquerque was a good idea. Well, there were those guys after him. Those *cholos*! So, he kept a little of their weed. So what? It wasn't like their beaner cousins in Mexico couldn't bring them tons more. He left that thought behind and dragged his feet toward the sagging door.

He was suddenly conscious that a car passing on the highway was slowing down. Fuck! Someone was driving in here. That stupid Ellie! She wasn't supposed to come back in the daytime. Then he thought maybe it wasn't her. He looked around for a hiding place. Not in that stinkin' house with the spiders and bugs. He dropped his sleeping bag and thrashed through the weeds to crouch behind a partially collapsed wall of the house.

The sun got hotter and hotter as he waited, and he had to take a leak. A fly buzzed in his ear and he swatted at it, then dropped his hand as he realized his chains were clinking together. He got on his hands and knees and tried to peer around the corner without making any noise.

A woman was walking along the crummy driveway, looking around at the trees and sky as though they were the most wonderful things she had ever seen. He guessed she hadn't heard him, or she would have run away. What kind of stupid woman comes to an old deserted place like this alone? She kept coming, closer and closer to his hiding place. Wait a minute? He knew her. He had seen her at the B&B by the river. He and Ellie had hidden in an arroyo one afternoon and watched to see if they would have a chance to get in and go through the guest rooms. What a waste of time! The bitch who ran the place never left, as far as he could tell.

She turned toward the so-called house now. He pulled back and froze. If he hadn't already been sweating like hell, he would have sweated now. Could she see him? She was looking around, turning around and checking the bushes on either side. Fuck! Now what? She was actually backing toward him, looking from side to side. She was just asking for it!

With a groan, he jumped up and wrapped both arms around her. Instead of standing still and begging to be released, as he expected, she immediately threw herself from side to side. Rusty tightened his grip, but she struggled to free her arms, at the same time kicking back, striking his shins with the heels of her boots. Then she screamed, "Let me go. Help, somebody!"

Rusty struggled for breath. "Shut up! No one can hear you anyway." He attempted to throw her to the ground, but she braced her legs and stayed on her feet. He couldn't think. What was he supposed to do now that he had her? She stepped to one side and drove an elbow into his belly. With an "oof," he loosened his arms, and she twirled out of his grip.

While he was still bent over, she started racing back up the trail.

"No way, bitch!" he yelled and tackled her on the path. They fell into a puddle, dirty red water splashing over them. She pulled free again and reached for a tree branch lying on the ground. He struggled to his feet but once again she was ahead of him. She jumped up and turned with the big stick in her hands.

"Keep away from me," she panted, waving the branch in front of her.

He sat back down in the puddle. Unbelievable! He'd gotten beat up by two women in one week. This one was kind of old, too. But fuckin' strong! This was way too much trouble, and he was ruining his jacket. "Okay," he said. "Okay. Don't hit me."

"Stay back or I will." She gripped the piece of wood like a baseball bat now, revolving her wrists as though ready to swing.

"Don't move," she said, and started to sidestep around him. Still sitting in the puddle, he swiveled to keep her in view but made no move to get up.

Just as she was nearly in the clear, he said, "I know your friend didn't do it."

He could tell that caught her by surprise. She dropped her guard, and at that, he sprang to his feet, grabbed the club, and threw it as hard as he could. He heard a splash as it landed in the river.

"Fuck it," he wheezed. "I'm sick of this. I'm not going to hurt you. I want to talk to you." It pissed him off that she didn't even look out of breath.

"Funny way to introduce yourself," she said, all the time edging closer to where she had left her car.

"No, really. Wait. What's your name? I know you're a friend of the lady at the B&B. And I know she's in deep shit right now. I can help her, but you have to help me."

He feigned attention on the state of his jacket, flicking drops of red water off the leather, watching her from the corner of his eyes.

"How do you know anything?" she asked.

"I have friends," he said, swiping a hand over the stubble on his scalp. "My girl friend, Ellie. She brings me food and stuff. She hangs around the Bath House and the bar and hears people talk."

She really looked interested now but continued to back away. "So, how do you know Lena's innocent?"

"I was there that day. I saw her just before they all started screaming 'murder.' She was in the front room, just for a second. She wasn't near the tubs. She would've had to kill that lady by remote control."

"How could you just stand around watching her? Where were the attendants?"

He shrugged. "I have a place where I can watch—" Uh-oh. Check that. She didn't need to know he watched the women undress sometimes. "The ladies that work there leave all the time. They hang towels outside on the line, go to the bathroom, clean the tubs. I've gone through that Bath House a hundred times, and no one saw me. The back door doesn't close right, so I can get in. Sometimes, Ellie helps me. People get zoned out in their tubs or when they're wrapped up. That's when they forget and leave their stuff around. If you're fast, you can be in and out and no one knows. We watch people." Yeah, he thought, so we can rip them off. They're all so dumb.

She still looked ready to sprint down the lane, but he could tell she was hooked.

"What do you want from me?" she asked.

"You're the marshal's girlfriend. I seen you two together. Before they started on your friend, I was their best suspect. Tell him I didn't do it either. Put in a good word for me."

She laughed. "I have no way to know if that's true. You just said you sneak around the Bath House without being seen, and you as much as admitted you steal things there. You could have strangled her and slipped away."

He tossed his head back and forth in frustration. "But I didn't *do* it. Do I look like I strangle people?"

Her reply was quick. "You almost strangled me. You didn't get off to a good start here, you know."

"I know. I panicked. I'm on probation for burglary, that's all, and they want to get me for this murder." He tried to look like he felt bad. "I'm sorry. I wasn't thinking. I just grabbed you, but I wouldn't really hurt you."

She actually relaxed her arms. That was a good sign, he thought.

"Why didn't you tell the marshal or the sheriff all this before?"

Fuck! Was she retarded? "Because I was denying everything, told them I wasn't there, didn't go near the place, didn't steal anything. I couldn't say I *saw* anybody there."

"Okay, then why change your mind now?"

"Because I'm sick of living out here alone in this stupid mess of a house, staying awake all night with things crawling on me in the dark." Maybe he needed to let her know he didn't have to do this. "Anyway, I figure my dad's lawyer can get me off the burglary rap. I want to go back to living in my car."

She gave him a strange look at that. What? Like she never heard of anyone living in his car?

"If you come with me to Carlton, to the marshal, and tell him what you told me, that may look good for you. I can't speak for him. If this lawyer is as good as you say, maybe he can use it to help you."

"Okay, let's go." He started toward the car, and she took several steps back to let him pass. When he stopped abruptly and turned, she was just a few inches behind him.

"I know one other thing that might help your friend. I'll tell if the marshal thinks it will help me. When I was getting away after the lady's body was found at the Bath House, I saw someone else sneaking around. Coming out the back door. And I saw this same person down by the river the night the second lady got killed. I saw your friend with her, too. You know who it was? The butch dyke. The one with the horns on her truck. That bitch who beat me up."

CHAPTER 18

When Amelie and Rusty arrived at the marshal's office, only the clerk was there. In her eagerness to get Rusty and his revelations to Carlton, Amelie had forgotten her muddy clothes, dirty face and disheveled hair. She realized the effect of her appearance when the clerk gasped as they entered. Amelie, speaking quickly to allay the young woman's anxiety, said, "Hi, Tami. Don't worry. I'm okay. Just had to dig my car out of the mud." She brushed dried clods from her shirt. "It's very important that we see the marshal. Can you tell me where he is?"

"He's in Reno, at a conference. Won't be back until Wednesday." Tami rose from her secretarial chair when she caught sight of Rusty and vaguely waved her hands. "Are you sure you're all right?"

Amelie assured her everything was under control. The clerk then picked up what Amelie recognized as the manual she had left with her a month ago. "In that case, could I ask you—"

"Not right now, Tami. I need to finish something first. Could you find one of the deputies and ask him to come over here, please." Carlton's deputies worked only on weekends, when the most traffic passed through the village. As far as Amelie knew, they hadn't been trained in interrogation, but either could take a preliminary statement. She wanted to get Rusty on record while he was in the mood to talk. He was fidgeting near the door, looking like he might bolt at any minute.

"Buy you a Pepsi, Rusty?" Amelie asked.

He brightened at this and sat in one of the cheap yellow plastic chairs that constituted a waiting area. Amelie got a can from the vending machine outside on the porch. From another vending machine, she bought two bags of Cheetos. That ought to hold him for a while, she thought.

While he stuffed orange things into his mouth, she paced the small office, tapping her fingers on the door frame whenever she passed. Finally, one of the deputies, Felix Jaramillo, rolled up in his own car. He got out and paused to stretch and scratch before mounting the creaky steps. He had to be in his sixties, but his lanky frame showed only a slight trace of pot belly. With poorly cut gray hair curling out from under his Stetson, he looked like the cowboy he still was on occasion when he worked the spring and fall round-ups on the Baca.

"Hi ya, Amelie. What's going on?"

"Felix, this is someone you may have met already." She gestured at the boy, who was wiping greasy fingers on the legs of his jeans. "Say hello, Rusty." This is like training a two-year-old, she thought. "He has something important to say about the murders, and since Carlton isn't here, I want you to take a statement."

"Well, Amelie, I don't know. Usually Carlton does that, or we call the county. Maybe I should check with one of the boys in Bernalillo, see if they can come out."

Rusty, having finished his snack, started toward the door. "Looks like this isn't a good time right now," he said genially. "I guess I'll come back later."

Felix had been corralling drunks and petty miscreants for a long time. With a speed that belied his easy-going manner, he blocked the door. "Just a minute, young fella. We haven't finished talking about this yet. Why don't you sit back down and let me make a phone call."

Rusty strolled to his chair, trying to act nonchalant, and Amelie stepped outside to buy him another bag of Cheetos.

Upon consultation with the sheriff's office, Felix learned that no deputies were available, due to a fatality accident on Hwy. 550. He was to take a statement and instruct Rusty to remain in the jurisdiction. Getting an address from Mr. Cooke, as Felix began to call the young man, was the first sticky question. They finally agreed that Rusty would park his car at San Antonio Campground near the junction of Hwy. 126 and Hwy. 4 for the next two weeks. If he was needed for further questioning, either a deputy or the Forest Service law enforcement ranger could find him there. Amelie followed the conversation closely and was gratified to hear that Rusty repeated the story he had told her almost verbatim. No changes. No surprises.

As it turned out, Rusty's old beater station wagon was parked across the plaza. He sprinted away, hoping to find Ellie in the library. Amelie called goodbye to his retreating figure. She trusted her intuition, but a tiny doubt niggled at the back of her mind. What if he was lying, trying to make himself look good by appearing cooperative? Too late she realized that he hadn't explained how he had one of Maria's necklaces. The doubt deepened. Had she just helped a killer?

Resisting the urge to scrub the seat where Rusty had been, Amelie wearily got back in her car and headed south to the Krazy Kokopelli. She found Lena in her customary spot in the kitchen, making her famous granola. The two women embraced for a long minute, Lena wiping away tears as she released herself.

"I think I suffered temporary insanity, Am. I couldn't even think straight when Carlton called to say he had to take me in for questioning. I know he hated to do it, and I made it so hard for him."

"He'll get over it, Lena. I think this all came out just the way he planned, and I have some new information for him that may help you, too. Before I tell you about that, I want to hear what Walter said when you told him."

Lena smiled, and her face softened. "He's been wonderful. He's not shocked. He's not going to leave me. Hard as it is for me to believe, he still loves me. He said he fell in love with the woman he met five years ago, and that wasn't the same woman who was a wild young thing in Seattle." She pressed her face in her hands, then looked up. Dark circles below her eyes gave her thin face a gaunt look. "I still wish he didn't know. The good news is to him it's all water under the bridge, gone, done, over with."

Amelie knew she was right. Walter would never bring it up; indeed, he might soon forget the whole thing. He truly lived in the moment; events from far in the past didn't gnaw at him. Lena, however, was another story. Amelie believed that the energy Lena invested in trying to put the past behind her ensured that she was never free of the shadow of her youth.

"Lena, those days *are* gone, and you are a different woman. Those of us who love you will never let any of that make a difference. I'm glad the secret is out. Having secrets isn't healthy. Surely you learned that in some AA or ACOA group or something."

"Yeah, maybe that will work for me someday. I hear what he says, that he forgives and forgets, but I can't make it compute. Too many family feuds in my formative years, I guess, where nobody ever let go of any insult or transgression." She put a baking pan of granola into the oven.

Amelie said, "With Carlton, it's different. He doesn't forget, but he doesn't hold a grudge. He just takes the slights to heart. He earnestly wants everything to be all right. I guess that's the difference. He can't let go until it's right – in harmony. He seeks balance."

Lena looked amused. "I thought you didn't care anymore, were on to the next conquest. The Russian police officer. Or, have you moved on from him, too?"

Amelie pondered for a moment before answering. "Police officer? Why do you call him that?"

"The way he questioned me at your house. So methodical and persistent. I can't believe he hasn't done that professionally. By the way, did I convince him of my innocence?"

"As a matter of fact, you did. Remember, though, he has a Ph.D. in Computer Engineering, not Criminal Justice. He says he just has a scientific mind. He's developed quite a theory, which Carlton was not eager to hear, I might add." Amelie expounded on Ivan's analysis of Lena's non-criminal personality. "But that's not all. Listen to this." She told Lena of her encounter with Rusty and his willingness to testify that she couldn't have killed Maria.

Lena was dubious. "Will they really believe him? An admitted thief, living in his car?"

"What reason would he have to make up lies to protect you? He would only lie if it would benefit him in some way."

"I hope you're right." Lena went into the kitchen and opened the oven to stir the granola. "Anything else?"

"Yes, although this isn't related to the murders. But it is interesting. I spent some time looking at old newspapers and learned that there was quite a land war here in the 1920s, and your house was a big part of it." She stretched her neck from side to side, trying to relieve the headache that had started after the encounter with Rusty. "Lena, can I have some aspirin?

Lena brought the aspirin bottle and a glass of water. Seating herself on the sofa, she listened intently as Amelie recounted the story. Amelie had started looking through old newspapers on microfiche, hoping for articles that would put a human face on the land transactions recorded in aged deeds. After wading through years of train schedules and local gossip, nearly dozing from boredom and eyestrain, a headline grabbed her attention: *Raiders Torch Jemez Ranch House.* This was the secret she was dying to share with Lena – that the original house on the KK property had not burned down from a careless accident. It was arson. According to reports in the *Albuquerque Journal*, night riders, caring nothing for anyone who might be sleeping inside, had actually pushed torches through the windows. And here was the next little piece she had been niggling on – one of the families had been living there. Parents and three children had managed to crawl out a back window and hide in the *bosque*. According to the newspaper accounts, the masked raiders had escaped, but suspicion rested heavily on disgruntled residents whose land had been taken unjustly, led by Jesus de Silva.

Lena jumped to her feet. "You mean Serafina's family?"

Amelie nodded. "Yes. They were once the biggest land owners here. Then they – and others over the years – lost most of it to the Swensons, which started a feud that became increasingly violent."

Having vigorously plumped all the throw pillows, Lena turned her attention to picking dead blooms off the geraniums under the big windows. "I'm confused. How did this happen?"

"Wait a minute." Amelie retrieved her briefcase from the stool at the breakfast bar, pulled out her notes and grinned. "Pay attention class; this will be on your final exam." Her tone became serious, and she glanced at the pages she held. "We go back to the original Cañon de San Diego land grant made to a group of pioneers from Mexico in 1798. The practice was to award land in two ways: individual families received small plots of a few acres, narrow strips extending from the river that allowed each family to have access to irrigation. In addition, all the families had the right to use a huge commons area for grazing and wood-gathering. This system was in place throughout the colonial territory of what is now New Mexico, Arizona, southern Colorado, and parts of Texas. It worked great until all that territory was ceded to the U.S. in 1848 under the Treaty of Guadalupe Hidalgo. The U.S. examined every claim, but the authorities simply could not conceive of commonly held land that was not owned by an individual."

Amelie recognized that Lena was definitely fidgeting now, straightening and re-straightening the magazines on the window seat. "Lena, please sit down. I'll try to hurry and get to the good parts, but this background is important. I think the undercurrents and enmities you feel in the valley today started about 150 years ago."

Lena poured two cups of coffee and carried them to the seating area near the fireplace. Amelie sat next to her, shed her sandals and propped her feet on a hassock. "In 1860, Congress approved the grant of 110,000 acres common land and 6,000 acres irrigable land to individual families." She looked up. "They were lucky. Most cases of disputed ownership went to a Land Claims Court, which denied all but a few who had what officials considered proper documents."

She turned to the next page. "But the 1860 grant from Congress wasn't the end of our local story. Over the next 50 years, various Swensons started picking up small parcels, pieces of the original family holdings that had been divided again and again through the generations. On top of that, the Swensons started claiming they owned part of the commons where they grazed huge herds of cattle. The final blow came when one of them fenced off a spring that was on the common land."

She smiled at Lena, who was, amazing for her, sitting still in rapt attention. "I told you it got better—and the saga continues. In 1904, heirs of the original settlers sued to get their land back. The court granted them 80 percent of their original holdings. The ringer is that the lawyer who represented them took half of that land in fees. And guess who the lawyer was?"

Lena thought for a moment. "A Swenson?"

"Bingo."

"But why?" Lena protested. "Why trust him after his family took their land?"

"That's not in the record. Probably he was the only lawyer around, and they had to have someone who spoke English and understood the American legal system. Maybe he convinced them he was different from his brothers and cousins. Who knows? What is clear is that he came out of the deal as the largest landholder in the valley."

"People do have long memories around here," Lena said. "So you're saying that the original *casa* on this land belonged to the de Silvas, then the Swensons took over, and years later the de Silvas and their friends burned them out." She tapped her lips thoughtfully with one long fingernail. "And Serafina is still obsessing on this?"

Amelie sighed. "I wish I could talk again to Carlton about her. He knows more about the recent family history." She paused, watching iridescent hummingbirds zoom to feeders hanging from the eaves. "He's gone until Wednesday. I'll come back next weekend. Maybe you and Walter can ask him more about this, ask if the land war is still going on?"

"Amelie, Wednesday is Feast Day at the Pueblo. Can you come back then and go with us? After all, Feast Day is a holiday around here. Consider it a holiday for you, too."

Amelie paused. "Okay, if I go home right now and get some work done, I can come back on Wednesday – if I can shake this headache." She left Lena with the admonition to get some sleep and let Walter help with whatever chores she might think could not be delayed.

By noon on Wednesday, Amelie, her aches and pains forgotten, was mesmerized by the drums, the heat, and the press of people in the plaza at Jemez Pueblo. She stood in the shade of a square flat-topped adobe house, newly mudded and restored, quite possibly one that had been there more than 300 years. She had learned on one of her first trips to the area that all Jemez people were forced by the Spanish into the existing village as part of the reconquest insanity following the 1680 Pueblo Revolt. For two hours, she watched as lines of dancers filled the plaza, moving rhythmically to the drum's beat and singers' drone. Amelie had been to Feast Days with Lena and Walter before, and she was always deeply touched by the ancient traditions played out before her.

All dancers, from gray-headed elders to toddlers, were dressed in traditional garb: women wore black *mantas* that bared one shoulder. Men's bare chests were rubbed with blue or brown paint to signify their moiety, squash or turquoise, sometimes referred to as summer and winter. Small downy feathers on the women's painted wooden headdresses moved slightly as they trod the dirt in time-honored steps; each footfall sent up a small puff of dust. Macaw feathers tied in the men's hair echoed the motion, while rattles in their hands and clusters of clacking deer hoofs tied at their knees resonated with the drums. All carried pine branches to symbolize life and growth; women held them in upraised hands, and they were banded onto men's upper arms.

Amelie stood respectfully behind the rows of folding lawn chairs lined up in front of the houses around the plaza, many holding colorful umbrellas as protection against the broiling sun. She enjoyed looking at the crowd almost as much as the dancers. The jewelry on display at these ceremonies was better than going to a gallery. She admired a huge silver and turquoise brooch pinned to the cotton dress of an elderly woman, who was being helped to a chair by a teenage girl with a glossy black braid down her back. Squeezed in a crush of onlookers that included many Anglo tourists, she nevertheless felt calmed and grateful for the privilege of being there. However, her legs were beginning to ache from standing.

Lena and Walter were talking with owners of a gallery in Placitas where Walter had shown his work. Amelie told them she'd return in an hour. She wanted to sit in the church to rest for a few minutes, and then take a quick tour of the vendors. Entering the church yard, she saw a woman dressed all in black coming out of the old adobe church. As she drew closer, she recognized Serafina and called out a greeting.

Serafina, as usual, stiffened and then stopped, waiting for Amelie to approach.

"Hi, Serafina. I've been hoping to talk to you. Do you have a minute?"

The woman nodded silently, wary cat eyes watching as though she expected an attack.

She is so weird, Amelie thought, but plunged ahead. "I've been looking at old newspapers, and your family's name came up. I guess your ancestors used to own the land that the Krazy Kokopelli is on. Is that right?"

Serafina narrowed her eyes, looking for all the world like she would hiss and spit at Amelie. Her voice was tight and hard, unlike the usually mellifluous tones she used to sooth the Bath House clients. "You have no right even to mention my family. Stay out of our business. We handle our own affairs. You are an outsider. Leave this valley. Go back to where you belong." She hurried by on the narrow flagstone path, and Amelie almost thought she heard a hiss as the fluttering black skirt brushed her legs.

Amelie stared at the retreating figure until the woman vanished behind a row of houses. Looks like I found a hot spot, she thought, then turned to slip through the heavy doors into the church's cool interior. The four-foot-thick walls had been newly painted white, and on either side, flanked by framed pictures of the Stations of the Cross, was a mural in traditional Jemez design. Lowering herself onto a hard wooden pew, she decided she was through trying to talk to Serafina. Her venomous anger was way out of proportion to the situation. Something is wrong with that woman, she thought, not for the first time. Carlton is right; she's mentally ill.

Sitting in the dim old church soothed her. When she felt relaxed and ready for the heat again, she stepped outside into the brilliant afternoon light. The dusty road that wound between small adobe houses was clogged with cars at every turn. The sound of the drums had again reached her when she felt a hand close on her upper arm. She turned to face Sage, who did not release his grip.

"Amelie, how are you? I just ran into Walter and Lena. It's nice to see someone else I know."

Amelie pulled away, realizing he was expecting her to be charmed by the congenial greeting and wondering why this man aroused such distaste. Maybe it was the smug arrogance of a man who thought he was irresistible to women. Maybe it was the bulging biceps of a muscle-builder, a trait she had never found attractive.

"Hi, Sage. Yes, I'm with them, but I wanted to wander around on my own for a while."

Apparently not understanding that this was a hint, he continued talking. "I haven't been back here since that awful day at the Krazy Kokopelli. I've been really busy. Had a lot of shows around the west and spent a nice month doing some more work in a little town in California you probably never heard of."

Amelie edged away, letting her eyes slide to a display of beaded earrings laid out on a card table. Oblivious, the man persisted.

"The gallery in Santa Fe just can't get enough of my stuff these days. They have a Saudi Arabian customer who wants more and more – I guess he has six palaces."

"That's nice, Sage." She ostentatiously lifted her arm to look at her watch. "I have to be going now. Enjoy the celebration."

"Yes, well listen. I'll be going through Los Alamos next week, then a stop in Santa Fe and back to Seattle. Let's have a drink."

"I doubt I'll have time for that, Sage. I have two new jobs coming up."

He responded as though she had agreed. "Okay. I'll give you a call."

Without a goodbye, she turned and walked briskly toward the row of vendors' booths, hoping he wouldn't follow. Glancing back as she rounded a corner, she no longer saw him.

After getting an overdose of silver and turquoise jewelry, succumbing only to a small pin with a pueblo incised on it, she started back to the plaza to join her friends at the appointed time. Searching through the crowd, she saw Walter's distinctive balding head, then her heart literally thumped when she recognized the cap on the tall man next to him. She stopped, thinking perhaps she should turn away, not ready to see Carlton again right now, not on this beautiful afternoon when she was feeling blessed by the ritual of drum and dance. This is ridiculous, she told herself. You *know* this man. You've *slept* with him. Why act like a teenager with a crush on the class president?

As she took a deep breath and pulled her shoulders back, another hand took her arm and a welcome voice said, "Take it easy. He can't hurt you in a public place."

"Hi, Lena. Where have you been?"

"Standing in line for the port-a-potty." She dropped her hand and fell into step with Amelie. "I told him you were here and that he had to behave."

They pushed through the throng, and Amelie greeted the men with what she hoped was suitable enthusiasm. Carlton obviously had taken Lena's admonition to heart and limited himself to a solemn nod. They had been deep into a serious conversation, and Walter now addressed Carlton. "You have to tell them."

Carlton hesitated, then spoke after Walter again urged him. "I just spent a week in Reno at a conference for small town law enforcement. I talked to a lot of marshals and, of course, mentioned that the biggest excitement around here in years was two murders." He lifted the cap to wipe his brow. "Turns out two of these guys had an almost identical crime; another marshal thought she remembered one some time ago. Same thing – woman strangled in water."

Amelie and Lena gasped in unison, then broke out in a jumble of overlapping questions. "Who were they?" "What towns?" "Did they catch anyone?"

Carlton held up a hand. "Whoa. Slow down – and not so loud. This isn't for the whole world to hear." They were pressed on all sides by the crowd watching the dancers. He glanced around. "Let's hold off until we're in private."

Lena grabbed his hand. "Then let's go. I want to hear this."

Pushing through to the edge of the crowd, Amelie heard Walter say, "Hello again, Sage . . . Ah, maybe next time. We're in kind of a hurry." They filed by the artist with quick greetings and nearly ran toward their vehicles parked on the edge of the highway.

Lena pulled up when she reached her truck. "This is far enough," she said. "No one can hear you. Say that again."

"Actually," Carlton said, "I don't have much more information." He leaned against the truck's tailgate and crossed his arms. "The marshals in Bluff, Utah, and Silver City, Nevada, told me they had similar crimes in the past, never solved. In both cases, the woman was strangled in a body of water – one in a stream, another at a B&B with a hot tub, just like at the KK. This happened five years ago and two years ago. The marshal at Winslow, Arizona, is new but said she had been looking at old files and thought she remembered something similar quite a while back."

Amelie wanted to ask a dozen questions, but she realized that the unspoken truce in place for this conversation easily could be broken. Fortunately, Lena was asking most of the questions that hovered on Amelie's lips.

"What are you going to do?" Lena asked. "You're going to tell the sheriff, aren't you?"

Carlton's face wore an expression of uncertainty. "I guess. They never seem to want to hear from me, but maybe they can follow up on this, even though it's pretty vague."

"Make them listen." Lena insisted. "This is a pattern. Maybe there are others."

Carlton nodded. "I asked all the marshals I met at the conference after I found out about those two, but no one else remembered anything like this. The county should be able to do a search – if they're willing to take this seriously."

Amelie could restrain herself no longer. "I can do that, too, through newspapers online. I'll see what I can find in the past – what? Ten years? I'll focus on small towns in the West."

Carlton looked as though he would object, but Lena threw her arm across Amelie's shoulders. "Thanks, pal. Maybe, with a little help from my friends, I'll get out of this mess."

Walter spoke in his usual laconic manner. "None of those towns are quite as small as Cañon Springs. This could be some weird coincidence. After all, I've been in both places in the past ten years. Bluff and Silver City both have – or had, they come and go so fast – unusually nice galleries for towns their size. I think Sage has shown in both those places, too."

Amelie shuddered. "Sage! He just grabbed me when I came out of the church. I know you like him, Walter, but I get – and I hate to use this word – bad vibes from him. Too bad he has an alibi for Maria's murder."

Walter eyed her. "Hey, Amelie. Sage is okay." Lena opened her mouth, then closed it again, and her husband continued. "What I'm saying is there's two of us right here who have been to those towns – and thousands of others. Like Cañon Springs, they try hard to attract visitors." He tapped his pipe against the sole of his Birkenstock sandal, then patted his wife's arm. "Just don't count on this as a great breakthrough."

Amelie returned to her car, leaving her friends at the side of the road still discussing the implications of this news. Glad for a chance to do something concrete to help Lena, she was eager to start her Internet search. An early appointment in Red River tomorrow meant she would have only a few hours to get started tonight.

As she settled behind the steering wheel, she felt a lump beneath her leg. Shifting her weight to slide a hand across the seat, she pulled out a strange figure, small enough to fit in her palm. Made of the familiar red mud, the clearly female shape was pocked with tiny holes. "What in the world is this?" she muttered. "I'm sure I locked all the doors."

She put the car into gear, then a frisson of fear ran down her spine. Maria had spoken before her death of being hexed, of finding an evil charm, according to the gossip Lena had gathered. Was this what the dead woman had found at her house? And were there others? She eyed the figurine with increasing horror. She didn't want to touch it, or have it near her. She rolled down the window, preparing to throw it as far away as she could. Then she stopped. She had to save this to show Carlton. Jumping from the car, she opened the trunk and wrapped it in an old plastic grocery bag. She was acutely aware of it being there all the way to Los Alamos.

At home, Amelie sped through the packing routine she had honed to twenty minutes over the past few years. After a quick look at the notes taken when she had accepted the job in Red River, she settled at the computer to start searching for crimes involving strangled women. Since Carlton had encountered two similar crimes in small towns, she started with a search for small-town newspapers. She looked for Bluff, which apparently did not have its own newspaper. The nearest town of any size was Blanding, and going back five years in the archives of the weekly *Blanding Voice*, she found an article about a woman murdered in a hot tub at a Bluff motel. The follow-up stories got shorter and shorter throughout the month, then she could find nothing more. Silver City had a monthly paper which featured its only major crime in a decade prominently on the front page of the July edition for that year. Then, a short article in the next month's issue said no new leads had been uncovered. Road atlas in hand, she cast around for other towns of like size. Randomly checking a few made her realize the enormity of her task. She had to identify the town, search to see if it had a newspaper, go to the nearest town large enough for its own press to search again, finally going back as many years as they had archived on line. This was impossible!

She got up and stretched, walking into the kitchen for a glass of iced tea. As always in the mountains, the night-time temperature was at least 30 degrees cooler than in the daytime. She stepped onto her deck and enjoyed the slight breeze lifting from the canyon.

Back in her office chair, she tapped a pencil on the edge of the desk while she thought of another approach. Walter had said both the towns where murders had occurred had outstanding art galleries. She would go in from that angle, searching for galleries in small towns in the Four Corners states of Colorado, Utah, Arizona and New Mexico. That still produced a daunting list and, she glanced at the clock, it was already 10 p.m. She could only give this a couple more hours. Doggedly, she started down the Arizona list. Carlton had mentioned Winslow, but the *Mail* only had a couple of years back issues on-line. After another hour, she slammed her palm on the desk in frustration. This was going nowhere.

She couldn't let go of the idea Walter had planted that there was a connection to the arts scene. Walter had posted a website to market his glass sculptures. Absently, she clicked onto it to see what photos he had up this month. Also listed were all his one-man shows for the past ten years. That gave her an idea.

She racked her brain for Sage's full name. Maybe he had a website, too. Sagittarius something, she thought, and added "paintings" to her search terms and eliminated astrology, to screen out thousands of hits on that topic. And here he was. In addition to photos of his work, the page included an extensive biography and a half-dozen photos of him: working out with weights, at his easel, celebrating his first Los Angeles opening with a starlet on each arm. She realized how his overweening ego was another factor that put her off. She didn't understand how Walter could overlook the man's constant need to talk about himself. She clicked a link and scanned his list of shows. As Walter said, he had been at Bluff and Silver City and – her hand froze on the mouse – the dates were the same as the murders there. For the first time, she noticed that the murders – four if you counted the two in Cañon Springs – all were committed in July. Had to be coincidence, but she could check it out. Where had Sage shown last July? She found it on the list, Dolores, Colorado, a tiny town in the southwest corner of the state. She searched for their newspaper. Yes! There was a story on a murder on July 15; a young woman had been found apparently drowned in McPhee Reservoir, and police were investigating it as a suspicious death. Next week's issue had more details about the victim, but no further information on the crime itself. On impulse, she emailed the gallery owner to confirm Sage's appearance at the opening.

She jumped up to pace around her small house. Sage! She knew she had good reason to dislike him. This was the lead they'd been waiting for. Her grandmother clock chimed midnight, and she returned to her office, forcing herself to shut down the computer. Sage had been in the vicinity of five murders committed in pretty much the same way. Of course, Walter had been around for four of them, maybe all. She didn't remember if he had ever shown in Dolores. If it weren't so late, she could call to ask for the name of other artists to use as a cross-check. The block to accusing Sage was his clear-cut alibi for Maria's murder; he had solid witnesses putting him at the bar.

Her eyes fell on the plastic bag containing the strange little figure she had found in her car. Thinking she might have time to research that, too, she had brought it into the office. She gingerly opened the bag, then snapped it shut. Looking at it disturbed her in some undefined way, although she would never admit she believed in curses or hexes or whatever they might be called.

Amelie reached for the telephone, then pulled back her hand. She couldn't call Carlton in the middle of the night with her suggestion of a link between Sage's showings and the murders plus news of a scary little mud doll. He had made it clear he didn't want her help. She needed irrefutable proof. Packing her laptop into its case, she placed it with her briefcase and overnight bag by the front door. She could continue searching tomorrow night, after the training. By the time she returned from Red River, she would find substantiation if it was there. Her gut told her she was on the right track. Two days from now, Carlton would have all the evidence he needed to take to the county sheriff—if she could get him to listen. She would give him no choice. He would have to talk to her.

CHAPTER 19

Sage sat in the dark at the end of Walnut Street, occasionally flicking ash from his cigarette through the open car window. Only the front porch of Amelie's duplex was visible from his vantage point, but she could not arrive from either direction without his seeing her car.

He was excited, looking forward to the night to come. Time to try something a little more challenging. The old routine was getting boring. His pelvis twitched, and he shifted restlessly in the cramped seat, constricted by the steering wheel. He touched the outline of the knife strapped to his belt. The women in his past flowed through his mind. He watched as though in an old-fashioned newsreel as a parade of bare bodies floated by. The announcer calls their names in a strident show time voice: Miss Silver City, Miss Dolores, Miss Cañon Springs. The camera moves in close to their vulnerable soft necks, panning up to their eyes, first surprised then dark with terror as his hands press tighter and tighter while he plunges into them. In some of the scenes, he shows them the knife before he leaves his mark. Then the water washes away the blood. Always best in the water. Keeps things so much cleaner.

Headlights interrupted his trance, and he straightened up enough to see through the windshield. A car came slowly toward him, then swung to the curb. Headlights cut off. The driver's door opened, and in a few quick strides, Amelie Jameson was inside her apartment. She slipped through the door so quickly he knew that she had the key ready in her hand. He sat erect now, no chance of his prey turning back to see the dark car at the end of the street. Even if she did, so what? She had no reason to identify his vehicle. Her dislike for him was quite obvious.

That was one factor that would be different. She was someone he knew and been attracted to – and spurned by. No one else had done that. None of the others had wanted anything but his attention, if not his affection.

Affection. That was Maria. Always trying to be "in sync," to commune. Yet, despite the New Age patter that drove him nuts, he had felt kindly toward her. She never questioned, never passed judgment. She had her little flings from time to time, he knew that. That's why he kept her. That little streak of independence intrigued him, just a tiny portion of her personality out of his control, briefly. He could always reel her in. For the past three years, she had come to him whenever he asked. And whatever he asked of her, she would do.

Sage needed Maria there waiting when he returned from his trips, and she accepted without question the reasons he gave. He told her he was stressed out from the intensity of shmoozing with gallery owners and patrons, being the gentle, wry artist for prospective buyers who would be able to say, "Oh, yes. I met him. So sensitive!"

Following one of his journeys to a small western town, he fairly sizzled with energy that he needed to dissipate. Coming home to Maria, claiming her pliant body as his own, helped ease the feverishness. Each of his encounters with other women was like an orgasm, *was* an orgasm, but instead of collapsing, he felt renewed surges of strength. As a younger man, he always had several girls on the string, sometimes having two or three in bed with him at once. He guessed he was mellowing in his 30s, but Maria alone had satisfied his need for someone at home whenever he wanted her. Now she was gone, her life choked off like the others. He still felt enraged when he thought of her going to another state without telling him, forcing him to discover where she was. Intolerable!

Lights had gone on in the bedroom and kitchen. He knew which rooms because he had checked out the duplex several times in the past two weeks – arriving at different hours of the day and night – watching first to see which neighbors were gone and who might come and go when he was prowling around. Her office light had been on until midnight day before yesterday, but last night she hadn't come home. Business or pleasure, he wondered? He hadn't entered the apartment, although he had tested all the doors and windows. Amelie was careful to lock up when she was away.

The kitchen light flicked out, and the bedroom light dimmed. Sage slid from his car and melted into the shadow of a cottonwood in front of the duplex. Apparently Amelie wasn't reading in bed tonight. Once he had crept close through the shrubs under the bedroom window. She locked up but didn't always lower the blinds. He had seen her spotlighted by a reading lamp, absorbed in a book, bare shoulders gleaming, sheet pulled up to barely cover her nipples. He could have pressed his nose to the glass without her knowing, but he had kept a discreet distance and withdrawn without a twig snapping.

Tonight he again congratulated himself on his ability to move with stealth. He headed toward the canyon, eyes adjusted to the dark, going downhill 30 feet before turning to climb to the back of his quarry's residence. A hot tub on the back deck was screened from the neighbors by a rickety coyote fence of irregular *latillas*, the thin trunks of young aspen used for ceilings as well as fencing. Now that he thought of it, the screen was very similar to the one at the Krazy Kokopelli. He crouched in the dark shadow of the deck and braced himself to keep from slithering down the steep slope and tumbling into the canyon. In a minute, he heard the sliding door open and shut, then the scuff of the hot tub cover being removed. Finally, his ears knew what his eyes couldn't see: she had slipped naked into the hot water. He heard a long sigh. His pelvis twitched again.

Taking his pleasure in a place like Los Alamos would be another new factor this time. He preferred the special problems posed by small towns. The law enforcement officers invariably were underpaid and less trained than their urban counterparts, so they weren't an obstacle to his doing what he wanted. The high degree of difficulty came from the very nature of a little community. Everyone was always checking on everyone else, either from neighborliness or spite. In those circumstances, to move around invisibly brought out the best in him. Tonight, he was mastering an unfamiliar milieu.

So slowly he barely felt himself move, Sage shifted until he could see through a gap in the fence. The scrape of a match thrilled him for now he knew he would have a candle-lit view through the narrow opening. Yes, there she was, head thrown back to rest on the hot tub rim, throat exposed. Inviting. He nearly jerked with excitement, but kept himself in check. Even so, she lifted her head and appeared to look directly at him, a slight frown tensing her forehead.

He held his breath. Yes, a smart woman, making intuitive leaps that could, just possibly, lead her to him. He knew she was the brains behind that hick marshal. Oh yes, Sage had been close enough to hear Carlton report his findings from other towns. He had watched the cluster of friends move off to the highway, standing in a tight knot, all talking at once. He had desperately wanted to hear more, but there was no way to get closer without being seen. At one point, he saw them all look at Amelie, saw Lena's arm fall onto her friend's shoulder. Amelie was going to do some detecting. He knew it. Of course, she would never be able to trap him. No woman could do that. But taking her, having her for himself would show the stupid marshal and his county sheriff pals just how helpless they were.

He re-focused on the figure in the spa. She had relaxed again and closed her eyes. Whatever sixth sense had alerted her to his unseen presence had been quelled, lulled by the hot water. If she were seriously worried, she would have gotten out and looked around or gone inside.

Yesterday, he had completed his routine preliminary tasks: researched the surroundings, assessed the risk, planned his moves. The other half of the duplex was occupied by a fifty-ish Chinese man who left promptly at 6 am and returned at 6 pm, always with a bulging briefcase under his arm. He kept his shades drawn.

He heard the water slosh and watched as Amelie stretched her arms overhead. Droplets glistened on her bare skin in the faint candlelight. His fingers flexed, and his legs tensed, ready to spring. She swept her hair up with one hand, and the nape of her neck gleamed. That movement caused the first stirring of his erection. He carefully placed one foot on the decking, set to vault up and pull open the flimsy gate. He had no doubt he could overpower her in an instant. She was an athletic woman, but from experience he knew that a sudden attack took even the fittest women off guard. And once he had his hands around their necks, no one yet had been able to defend herself. He anticipated the coming episode: heard her last gasp, saw the crimson lines blossom as he put his mark on her neck and breasts, tasted the salty tang of blood. With great deliberation, he placed his palms in front of his foot on the deck. Now!

A shrill ring cut into the night air and arrested his movement. Amelie hoisted herself to the edge of the tub and reached out of his line of vision, apparently picking up a phone that she had brought out with her.

"Hello, Ivan," she said. "No, I'm just going to bed. I have a lot to tell you, though. And thanks so much for helping get Lena out of here." She paused, listening to the caller. Sage turned the name over in his mind. Ivan? Amelie continued. "Yes, I know you have a theory, but I have more than that. I know who the killer is. Yes, that's right." She listened again. "No, I'm going to bed now. Let's meet tomorrow. I'll call you in the morning . . . Uhmmm. Good night."

Sage held his position, listening to her drop the cover back on the hot tub. The sliding door opened and closed; the lock clicked. Disappointment flooded through him in an overwhelming rush. Feeling nauseous from unreleased tension, he dropped from his crouch onto the rocky hillside. So, she thought she knew who the killer was. But what could she really know? He would have to act quickly, but not tonight. He must do it right, although the risk increased if she shared her supposed knowledge. Who was Ivan? Probably, she was cheating on the marshal with some Lab geek. Not that it wouldn't serve the cop right, but she should be punished for that. He had a lot of reasons to punish her – in his own way.

Sage crept to his car and slowly rolled down the street, where all the windows were dark now. He already had the germ of a new plan. She would, of course, show up again at the B&B, and he already had scouted that territory. That's where he'd wait for her next time. He almost laughed. Two in the same place! That'll really screw up the poor marshal!

CHAPTER 20

Amelie struggled to get out of bed. She had slept poorly the night before, even after a soak in the hot tub. Noises outside in the dark had repeatedly startled her awake, then when her heart had stopped thumping, she acknowledged familiar sounds: a car accelerating or gutters rattling in the wind. She sat at the edge of the mattress with her feet dangling, thinking about the day ahead. She had to get to Cañon Springs and tell Carlton what she had learned about Sage. Guilt at the work awaiting on her desk made her hesitate. Maybe she should call. No, she debated with herself, this had to be in person. Besides, he probably wouldn't accept her call. The fragile truce they had struck at Jemez Pueblo for the sake of Lena and Walter had barely lasted through the day. She recalled his look of disgust when she offered to research Sage's movements, could almost read his mind: Always thinks she knows more than I do. Always trying to take over.

She was halfway to Cañon Springs before she remembered that she had promised to call Ivan. She reached for her cell phone, then paused. Carlton deserved to hear this first. Ivan could wait – again. Negotiating the curves on autopilot, she rehearsed her speech to Carlton, mumbling to herself as she swept past the vast expanse of the Valle Grande and through the tall pines. Thunderheads were building in the north, towering white clouds which she knew by afternoon would roil and rise until the sky was gray and crackling with lightning.

By the time she came to a dusty stop in front of the marshal's office, she had refined her speech until the evidence sounded, to her, compelling. Her sweaty palms slid over the railing as she mounted the wooden steps.

Although the marshal's pickup was parked in front, Amelie knew before she reached for the door knob that only Tami was here. Music from an Albuquerque hard rock station blasted through the closed door. Carlton never would have permitted such unprofessional conduct in his office, and she deduced he must be elsewhere. When Amelie entered, she saw the young woman standing in front of a filing cabinet, back to the door, sheaf of papers in hand, hips swinging to the beat.

"Tami," she shouted. "Where's Carlton?"

No response.

She strode across the office and tapped the clerk's shoulder. Tami jumped and turned around, face breaking into a smile. "Hi, Amelie," she yelled.

Amelie reached out to turn off the radio and repeated her question. Tami reported that Carlton had taken a patrol car to drive to Bernalillo for a meeting, planning to return just in time to start his shift at noon, scheduled to end at 8 p.m. She didn't think he would have time to sit down and talk.

Obviously, Amelie's face revealed her dismay, and Tami grabbed her hand. "What's wrong? Do you need help?"

Amelie shrugged. "No, it's okay. I just wanted to talk to him. Please leave a message that I came by. Since I'm here, how are you doing with the program?" They spent the next hour going over the latest problems Tami had encountered, and Amelie discovered the files hadn't been backed up for two weeks. She felt she had snubbed the clerk the last time she asked for help, so now Tami received her full attention.

Finally, leaving Tami reeling from information overload, Amelie drove down Hwy. 4 to the Krazy Kokopelli. Lena had just pulled sheets out of the dryer, and they talked while putting clean linens on all the beds. Amelie couldn't hold back the information about Sage. She poured it all out – the coincidences of the gallery showings and murders being on or near the same dates and the similarity of the crimes to those in Cañon Springs. She told Lena how nervous she had been approaching Carlton's office.

Lena laughed. "You are spooked, aren't you? You're over-reacting. He's hurt and defensive, but he hasn't stopped caring about you. When you left the Pueblo, I saw him watch your car until it was out of sight. If you gave even the slightest signal, he'd be back."

Amelie sighed. "That's probably true, which is why I have to be so careful not to give the slightest signal. I can't play cat-and-mouse with him. I've learned that much. If I'm not ready to be monogamous, to be 'his woman,' then I should stay away, except I have to talk over this Sage business."

A sudden blast of wind shook the large house and twigs skittered across the roof. The distant rumble of thunder that had been in the background since Amelie arrived was now a series of sharp cracks marching closer.

In the Zuni Room, Lena asked, as she had many times before, "What do you want, Amelie?"

Not wanting to muss the freshly made bed, Amelie slumped to the floor, back against the wall. "That's the problem. I don't know. Right now, I feel determined to work through this problem of the murders. Somehow I want to help Carlton on this, even if he doesn't want my help. I feel in love with him whenever I look at him, then I go away and I think how different we are and how much I'd have to change my life to be with him. At the same time, I want to change. I can't keep going on this way." She plucked idly at the carpet. "Why is this relationship so hard to figure out? Why can't I be organized and efficient and think this through like I do a problem at work – or this murder mystery?"

Lena plopped down next to her. "You and I had similar experiences, although in very different settings. We both were on our own as teenagers, and we had to be tough and independent. But after those wild years in Seattle, I couldn't wait to settle down. You're still wild, in a sedate 30 year-old way. I found comfort and strength in marriage, despite all my insecurities. I know this sounds corny, but maybe you just haven't met the right guy." She bumped Amelie's shoulder with her own. "And speaking of, what about this Russian guy?"

"Ivan? I don't think I have any illusions about our relationship, such as it is. I'm interchangeable with the next woman to come into his life. For him, sex is like another routine in his exercise schedule, which is fine. That's the way I want it. The sex was great, and, by the way, it was only once. I've turned him away since then. He called last night, but I haven't seen him in over a week."

Lena rose and dusted off the seat of her jeans, a superfluous gesture from anyone sitting on her spotless floors. "I have to run to Bernalillo and pick up some groceries, which won't be too much fun in this storm. Want to come along?"

Amelie declined. The trip to the nearest supermarket took forty-five minutes, and she wasn't in the mood to spend more time in a car. Lena grabbed her purse and a list off the counter. "Make yourself at home." As her pickup roared away in a spurt of gravel, a tremendous crash split the air. Huge raindrops splattered the ground. Within a minute, the downpour settled to a steady drumming on the metal roof, interspersed by the flash and crackle of lightning strikes on the mesa above.

Amelie wandered into the living room, picked up a copy of *New Mexico Magazine* and flipped through the pages. In a few minutes, despite the storm booming around her, she closed her eyes and dozed. She awoke with sudden fear clutching her throat. A dark figure stood by the sofa, unmoving as a pillar of stone. Amelie gasped and sat up so fast her head swam. The figure remained rigid and solid, not a dream, and when her vision cleared, she recognized Serafina.

"My god, you scared me to death!" Amelie squinted into the light. The storm had passed, leaving streaks on the windows. The sun was low, nearly ready to drop behind the mesa.

Serafina, a silhouette against the dying light, nodded and spoke in what seemed to Amelie, in her befuddled state, to be a disembodied voice. "Lena always told me to come in when she's away. I brought some tea. It's in the tin on the kitchen counter."

Amelie rubbed her forehead. "Uh. Thank you." She shook herself.

The voice said, "Could I make you some tea?"

Fuzzy-headed though she was, Amelie thought this an extremely odd offer. The woman had cursed her at their last encounter. She moistened her dry mouth. "That's very nice, Serafina, but I think I'd prefer something cold right now. I'm still half asleep. I'll just go wash my face. Won't you sit down?"

But Serafina was gliding toward the door, pushing something into a deep pocket in the long black skirt. "I will return when Lena is here. Have a nice day."

She was gone like a wraith, and Amelie sank back into the sofa. She rubbed her eyes and went into the bathroom to splash cold water on her face. Then she wandered outside.

The grass was wet and steaming, and the sound of the river was notice-ably louder than when she had arrived earlier in the afternoon. She strolled along the path, in and out of shadows cast by looming cliffs, savoring the cleansed look of bright green cottonwood leaves. She saw the river had come up at least six inches, colored the rusty red that followed every cloudburst. Rocks and branches tumbled and clattered in the rising water. She followed the path until she was out of sight of the KK, heading south in the direction of the fishing access park. She thought about Sage, considered by so many to be charming and cosmopolitan. A sliver of doubt pierced her resolve. Could such a man – an artist and presumed intellectual – be a serial killer?

A rustle in the willows warned her that someone was coming, but she turned too late. Something looped around her neck. Reflex brought her hand up, and she slid fingers into the space between the ligature and her throat. The pull on her neck tightened, forcing her head back. She flailed behind her, bending and twisting to throw the attacker off balance. Sounds of panting, maybe her own, filled her ears.

Her first idea was that this was Rusty, gone nuts again, because the sudden assault from behind was the same. No, not Rusty, she had identified the killer: Sage. The thought of his arrogance fueled her resistance. Swing-ing around with all her strength, she knocked them both into the river. One of her hands remained caught, trying to protect her throat. As she crashed hard onto the rocks, the pressure loosened. Pain shot from her shoulder into her neck and down her arm. She scrambled to her feet, spitting out water, struggling for firm footing. Looking over her shoulder as she fought to reach the river bank, she glimpsed a black-hooded figure reaching for her. She tried to call out. The intent was there, but no sound emerged from her constricted throat. She stumbled, and the unseen assailant regained a grip on the cord, and dragged her mid-stream. The strangling took hold again.

Once more, Amelie lost her footing on the slippery stones and went down, wrists and knees jarred by the fall. She felt her head being pushed toward the raging water. She reached behind for a hold on the attacker. Her hand grabbed nothing but air. Bruised and weakening, she felt her body failing her, arms drooping, legs buckling. The turmoil of water pushing against her grew wilder, and then she was face down into the current. Panic engulfed her, and she attempted to raise her head, desperate to take in air. She gulped and swallowed water. Heaving gasps shook her body. She couldn't breathe! Water rushed around her as though she were another boulder in the river's path. Her strength slipped away, and she went under.

"Hey, Amelie!" Rough hands grabbed her hair, yanking her head up. She retched, dredging up brown silt from her lungs, gagging again and again. She felt the grip on her head and feebly batted her hands at the other's arms. Helpless, she sagged, her strength completely gone. The voice sounded familiar but far away. "Come on, Amelie. Breathe! Atta girl!"

Amelie sucked in air with ragged breaths and with them came some understanding of what was happening. She was being rescued! She wasn't going to die in the muddy Jemez River, killed like the others by a maniac who seemed always to escape detection. She struggled to get her legs under her and fell again.

A sharp voice cut through the confusion that clogged her brain. "Police! Let go of her. Now! Put your hands up!" The rescuer's grip remained steady. The harsh voice again. "I said, let her go."

The hands fell away, and Amelie dropped again onto bruised hands and knees. The pain of smacking against the rocks brought clarity, and she was able to see who was speaking. Carlton stood on the bank, service revolver aimed at a woman standing knee-deep in the river, wet from head to foot. The woman had her hands half-way up, and her eyes darted from Amelie to Carlton. The marshal shifted the gun to his left hand, keeping an unwavering bead on the woman. He extended his right hand. "Hold onto me, Amelie. Can you get up?"

Amelie crawled toward Carlton and raised her hand to grasp his. He pulled her from the river with one swift motion while the level weapon never faltered.

"Carl – ," she croaked. Coughing, she tried again. "Carlton, no! She's not . . ." She collapsed in the muddy weeds, retching, tasting bile.

The woman in the river had recovered. "Look, buddy, don't point that gun at me! I'm the good guy here. Ask her." She pointed at Amelie, still sprawled at water's edge. "And could I get out of the water now?"

Carlton gestured with his gun, and the woman slogged to the river bank. He flicked a glance at Amelie, who shook her head up and down as vigorously as she could. She tried speech again. "That's right. She saved me. Jenny did. Someone tried to strangle . . ." She shuddered and broke off. Tears formed as she realized how close she had been to death.

Carlton lowered the gun and addressed Jenny. "I'm sorry. I saw the struggle, and it looked like you were trying to drown her." He knelt beside Amelie. "Are you all right? Of course, you're not, but are you injured anywhere?"

Amelie cautiously tested arms and legs, then sat down. "No, I'm okay, except that my neck really hurts. And my hand."

Carlton saw the welt circling her neck and the cuts on the inside of her fingers on the left hand. His jaw tightened. "Let's go inside and get you two dried off."

Jenny started to walk in the direction of the fishing access. "I don't think it's a good idea if I go in there. I'll just go home to change clothes."

Carlton laid a now-gentle hand on her arm. "I have to know what happened. You can go as soon as I take a statement." His shrewd instinct for people's needs, which seemed to apply to everyone but Amelie, made him say, "No one's there now. We'll just borrow some of Lena's towels."

The women dripped and shuffled up the path and into the mud room off the kitchen. Carlton raided the linen closet and came back with a pile of fluffy bath sheets, then left them to strip off their wet clothes. By the time they came into the living room, swathed in terry cloth, he had hot tea ready and waiting – licorice tea, Amelie's favorite. Tears started again as she recognized this act of thoughtfulness.

"I think we should go to the emergency room, Amelie," he said. "That was pretty rough. You need to get checked out."

Amelie held the warm cup in both hands. "No, I'm okay, just sore—like I've fallen off a cliff. I found some antiseptic for my fingers. Just let me rest. I don't want to go to the hospital."

Carlton, who seemed always to be biting back words today, looked worried, but he assented without further argument. "Then, let's hear what happened. Jenny, you first." He took a little notepad from his shirt pocket. The two women sat on the sofa where Amelie had napped just an hour ago; Carlton perched on an ottoman taking notes.

"I was just taking a walk along the river," Jenny began, sliding a sideways glance at Amelie, who didn't miss the look. Spying on Lena, she thought, but said nothing. She and Carlton could talk about that later.

"I saw someone dressed all in black, with a black hood over his head, come out of the brush and jump on Amelie," Jenny continued. "Then they fell and were thrashing around in the river, and I could see she was going down, so I jumped in. The other person ran away while I was pulling Amelie's head out of the water. I never saw his face. That's it." She waved a dismissive hand and started to rise.

Carlton extended his hands, palms down, and made a suppressing motion. "Whoa. Give me a description. Height? Hair color?"

Jenny sank back, sipped tea and considered. "Probably about my height and much slimmer. Everything was covered, so I couldn't see hair or skin color. He had what looked like a cord in his hand. He took it with him."

"Which way did he go?"

"Upriver, away from where I was parked."

Carlton persisted, but Jenny could add nothing to her account. He finally conceded she could go home and advised her that the county deputies would probably come by to interview her again.

When she had gone, he asked Amelie a series of questions about what she remembered. She had no description of her attacker, had barely glimpsed the black hood. Her brain seemed to be working again, and when he had finished his questions, she told him what she had learned about Sage. Carlton's lips compressed into a thin line, but he made no comment.

"Somehow he must have learned I was checking on him," Amelie said. "Do you think this is enough information to take to the sheriff? To arrest him?"

Carlton scratched his head. "I'm not sure, but I definitely want to ask him a few questions." The edge in his voice made Amelie look sharply at him, but when he continued, the tone was unemotional. "Problem is, I'll have to find him first. He could have driven over from Santa Fe, be half-way home by now."

The back door slammed, and Lena's voice called out. "I'm home. Dinner will be ready in an hour. Let's have a drink." She burst into the living room with a soda in one hand and two beers in the other. When she saw Amelie's attire, she back-tracked. "Oh, I'm sorry. I didn't know – I didn't mean to interrupt." She grinned. "But I'm glad to see you two made up."

Amelie grimaced, and Carlton blushed. "It's not what you think, Lena," Amelie laughed. "Bring those drinks over here, and we'll tell you the whole story."

Lena was in tears by the time Amelie had finished. "Carlton, go get him. He tried to kill Am. What are you waiting for?"

Carlton's reply was interrupted by the doorbell, and Lena went to answer. Amelie was shocked to hear Ivan's voice. Carlton stiffened and got to his feet. When Lena didn't return immediately with the unexpected visitor, Amelie surmised she was hurriedly telling him of the afternoon's event.

Her guess was verified when Ivan entered and walked directly to her, taking her hands in both of his. "You are not hurt? I have sorrow this has happened. I come to warn you, but I am not here in time." He shifted as though to sit beside her, but Lena deftly slipped in between them, ostensibly to offer Ivan a beer.

Carlton hadn't missed a word. "Warn her about what? What do you know?"

"I analyze evidence I have, all I have heard from Amelie. I come to her house this morning, but she is gone. I walk around, check windows to see if she is safe from intruder. I find footprints near deck, someone standing there many minutes, maybe hours, also under window. This is also confirmation of theory that . . ."

The door opened once again, and everyone jumped, on edge from the menace they felt around them, heightened by Ivan's tale. Walter entered, looking surprised to see all eyes on him. "Hi, everyone."

Lena grabbed his arm and dragged him into the living room. "Walter! Sage tried to strangle Amelie and drown her in the river. Just now! She barely survived!"

Walter slowly dropped his hat on the table and replied in his usual drawl. "What are you talking about, honey? I was just with Sage. We've been at the bar for the past two hours."

⚜ CHAPTER 21 ⚜

Everyone stared at Walter, jaws gaping. His verbal bomb had stunned them into near-stupor, so sure were they that Sage had been marauding outside just minutes before. Carlton reeled, instantly regretting that he had been so quick to accept Amelie's identification of someone she hadn't really seen. Walter spread his hands, palms up, in a gesture of surprise and apology. "What did I say?" Then he focused on Carlton. His normally languid voice hardened. "I know Amelie doesn't like Sage, but can't you give the guy a break?"

They released a collective breath, and exclamations and questions exploded around him. Carlton's sonar, always tuned in to Amelie, saw her put hands to her temples as though to wrench an answer to this new conundrum out of her brain. He moved to lay his hand on her shoulder. She leaned into him, and he saw she was near collapse.

He stood quietly, feeling the pressure of her body against his leg, staring sightlessly through the high windows at the glooming landscape outside. Birds chattered in the scrub oak, saying good night as dusk darkened the cliffs. The river tumbled noisily toward the Rio Grande, and Carlton wondered how long it would be before Amelie could hear that sound as comfort, not as threat.

He remembered last winter when she had terrible bronchitis and a raging fever. He had wanted to stay with her, make her chicken soup and place cold compresses on her forehead. Instead, she had kicked him out, told him to go home until she was fit company. But this was different. Turning decisively, he said, "Amelie, go borrow some of Lena's clothes and get dressed. I'm taking you to the hospital." He braced himself for the anticipated argument.

Her surprised look lasted only a few seconds. She coughed and put a hand to her throat. "Okay," she said and rose from the sofa.

Lena, apparently too intent on the enigma Walter had presented to notice her friend's change of attitude, cried, "Wait. You can't leave now. We have to figure this out."

Carlton met her eyes and shook his head slightly. She stammered, "Uhh. Well, maybe Walter and I should take her."

Carlton's eyes bored into hers, and she capitulated. Amelie had started shuffling toward the door. "Oh, all right. I'm coming, girlfriend. Let me help you."

Within twenty minutes, Amelie was seated in Carlton's pickup. She vaguely noted that neither Walter nor Ivan were in the big front room when she left, wearing a long skirt with elastic waistband and a loose cotton tunic. She had actually apologized to Carlton for the hippie look, explaining that these were the only things that would adapt from Lena's model-thin frame to Amelie's size 12. The face she turned to him was pale and strained.

"Does your neck hurt?" he asked.

She started to nod, then winced. "Yes, it hurts now more it did right after."

"Can you talk?"

"Yes, if I don't move anything but my lips." Her voice was husky.

They drove in silence as far as the Pueblo. As Carlton swung through the curves, his mind reverted to the sight of Amelie struggling in the river. Anger surged through him again. He frequently felt so frustrated that he wanted to strangle her himself. Now, faced with a very real threat, knowing she could have died, he wanted only to take care of her.

Several times he lifted his cap to run long fingers through his thick hair. In Amelie's presence, the habitual action made him conscious that he had missed a haircut appointment yesterday. Finally, he let out a breath on a long exhale and repeated the question he'd asked at the B&B, a desperate tinge to the words. "Who else could be after you, Amelie? If we eliminate Sage, who's left who wants to murder you?"

"Maybe a case of mistaken identity?" She tried for a sardonic tone, but her voice cracked and sank to a whisper. "I've been thinking of something that occurred to me weeks ago, Carlton. Something that seems highly improbable yet fits the facts." She took a deep breath, winced again. "What if we are dealing with two killers?"

Carlton erupted. "Two? What are the chances of that in this little valley?" He stopped. He was taking unfair advantage. She was not fit for combat. "I'm sorry, I interrupted. Keep talking."

"Thank you. You know I'd be yelling at you if it didn't hurt so much." She reached out and squeezed his hand that rested on the gear shift. He turned his palm over and cupped hers.

She continued, her words barely audible over the engine noise. "It appears we have two sets of unlikely circumstances. The first is that Sage has been in the location of five similar killings, including the two here. What are the odds that an innocent person would be in all those towns on the same day someone was murdered?" She touched her sore neck; when she continued, her voice was fainter. "The only other people that might possibly be on that circuit are fellow artists. With more time on the Internet and telephone I can find out who else had shown in those galleries on the same dates."

Carlton heard her inhale sharply as she crossed her legs. By now, she must be feeling bruises from every river stone. "Maybe you shouldn't talk, Amelie. Rest your throat. My turn."

He picked up the thread. "The other strange circumstance is that Sage, our current primary suspect, seems able to be in two places at once. When Maria was killed, he was in plain sight at the bar. When you were attacked, he was with Walter, again at the bar."

He pulled up in San Ysidro, the only stop sign on Hwy. 4 in 100 miles. As he accelerated onto Hwy. 550, he resumed. "Let's work from the assumption that you're right. Two killers, similar method. If you feel like talking again, I have a question for you. Think carefully. You saw both bodies. Did you notice any differences?"

He waited, glancing at her face in the dim glow of the dash lights. He knew she'd rather not dwell on the images of the dead women. Finally, she whispered. "Both had deep lines around their necks, like I would have if it weren't for Jenny." Her hand went again to the abrasion on her neck. "Maria's necklace was partially embedded in the flesh. I saw a little section of it glinting deep in the cut." She paused, took a couple of deep breaths. "The woman at the KK wasn't wearing a necklace. She had a deep cut around her neck and lines down to her breasts, like they were cut with a knife." She shuddered. "I didn't see lines like that on Maria."

Carlton nodded eagerly, as though he was encouraging a star pupil. "That's right. I noticed the same thing. A slight variation, although nothing to say the same person didn't feel like improvising." He swung into the left lane to make room for a gypsum truck coming down from a mesa-top mine. "Here's a couple of bits of information I shouldn't tell you, but I will. I have coffee with one of the county deputies now and then, the one who doesn't think I'm an idiot. He told me the results of the autopsies. They found traces of two herbs in Maria, valerian and betony, which would have made her drowsy. Nothing similar was found in the second victim. The other thing is that when I searched the cubicle where Maria was killed, I found a weird little doll, made of clay, wedged behind the pipes." He grimaced. "Those are the main strikes against me as far as the county goes, that I messed up both crime scenes. This doll is something they're keeping under their hats." After a brief inner debate, he decided to keep one fact to himself: the KK victim had been sexually assaulted.

Amelie straightened up, then groaned and gingerly touched her neck. "I didn't tell you!" He leaned toward her to hear the words. "I found one of those dolls in my car."

"You what?" Carlton shouted, and the car swerved as he turned to stare at her. "Why didn't you tell me?" Because you were avoiding her, stupid, he answered to himself immediately, and shutting her down every time she tried to speak to you.

Her hands fluttered up. "I was going to. I – " Her voice broke, and she choked.

"Ah, Amelie, I'm sorry. Don't talk anymore. We'll be there soon."

She fell back against the seat, and he noted with pleasure that her hand remained curled inside his. They were coming into Bernalillo, passing the fast-food franchises that lined the highway on the outskirts of the old Spanish town. Coronado and his troops had camped here in 1540 on the banks of the Rio Grande, near a thriving Indian village called Kuaua. Amelie had taken him to see the ruins, now a state monument. On a beautiful day last autumn, they had strolled along the paths among the ancient room blocks, then walked to a picnic spot near the river. He had lived here all his life and never bothered to visit this historic spot until she showed it to him. He squeezed her hand gently, which brought his mind back to the present.

Carlton mused over the doll he had found. The county had it now, if they hadn't lost it. He had asked Serafina about it that day of the first murder. She had given him one of her mystery looks and said it was nothing, a relic of the old days. He would ask if the deputies had questioned her about it.

He stopped at the Presbyterian Hospital emergency entrance, and they straggled into the fluorescent-lit reception area. Two hours later, he helped Amelie adjust her neck brace as she settled into the pickup. The diagnosis was severe contusions and multiple abrasions – no fractures. She had been given Motrin for the pain, and a week's supply of Robaxin, a muscle relaxant, was clutched in her hand. She slept, snoring lightly, for the entire drive back to Cañon Springs.

Carlton pulled off the highway at the turnoff to the Krazy Kokopelli. Amelie didn't stir. He watched her slack face for a few minutes, profiled in the faint moonlight. The woman was difficult, no doubt about that. Infuriating quite often. What was the hold on him? He sat quietly, trying to let go of his anger and frustration. The tenderness he always felt flooded through him, not from his head, not totally from his groin, but fully from his heart. She was his heart's desire, and he didn't know how to win her.

With a "harrumph" that even he recognized as old-fashioned, he shifted into first gear and drove away from the KK. He slowed to the required 25 mph through the Village, noting that Felix had parked the patrol car in front of the bar. He looked at his watch. Last call in a few minutes. He sped north, past house lights dotting the dark valley floor near the river, bracketed by black canyon walls. His little adobe sat near the river, a three-room house with a flat roof which he had patched innumerable times.

He opened the passenger door and slipped his arm behind Amelie's back, easing the other hand under her legs to nudge her out of the car. She moaned and mumbled, "What are you doing?"

"Amelie, I'm going to take care of you tonight." He tilted her to a standing position. "Let's go inside."

She groaned, her eyes flickered, closed, then drowsily opened in a blank stare. He couldn't tell if she knew where she was. He placed one of her arms over his shoulder, and with his support she stumbled into the house. He guided her to the bedroom. Lifting the dead weight of her legs onto the bed, he considered undressing her, then settled for removing her sandals. He tenderly drew a light blanket over her and kissed her forehead.

Carlton put his weapon in its customary place on the closet shelf. Then he softly closed the bedroom door and went into the kitchen to make a peanut butter and jelly sandwich. He had tried to get over Amelie, to cut his losses and move on. He knew local women considered him one of the best catches in the valley. He had dated quite a few, and contrary to Amelie's image of him as naïve and straight-laced, he had slept with several. Perversely, when he had started to date Amelie, who had made it clear from the start that she would be making no commitment, he had an urge to monogamy. Perhaps it was his time of life – thirty-eight years old, one failed marriage, a child he loved but had essentially lost when her mother moved to Michigan. At his age, he kept thinking, he should stop fooling around like he was twenty and pass the title of "most eligible bachelor" to someone else. He put the dishes in the sink and went into the living room to lie down on the lumpy old sofa fully clothed.

When the morning sun roused him, he went immediately into the bedroom. She was awake, staring at the ceiling, immobilized by the neck brace. "Good morning," she said without turning her head.

"Hope you don't mind that I brought you here," he said "Can I get you something?"

"One of those lovely pills, only cut in half. I want to be semi-coherent."

She continued to gaze at the ceiling, seemingly content to wake up in his bed. He thought of the mornings when he had been awakened by her stroking hands, arousing him as he swam up from the depths of slumber, laughing as he reached for her, smiling eyes holding his as they made love.

"And coffee," she added.

He was just filling two cups when she walked into the kitchen, concentrating on each step, body rigid. She settled gingerly onto one of four old wooden chairs set around a heavy square table. He set coffee and a glass of orange juice in front of her.

"I think I'll talk to Serafina's uncle, Luis" he said. "We've been friends since one of his grandsons and I were on the high school football team the year we went to state. He never missed a game. I think he can tell me about the dolls."

"I'd like to come, too. But the only clothes I have are the ones I slept in."

Carlton was startled. He actually hadn't planned to visit Luis today or to do anything today but watch over her. His fantasies had already projected a long day during which he solicitously brought her tea, and she was so grateful to him that they didn't have any arguments. Clearly, that fantasy wasn't in Amelie's plans.

"I doubt he'd talk to you anyway," he said, "and I hate to leave. Are you sure you'll be okay here alone?"

Of course, she dismissed that. "Yes, go on. I'll call Lena to come get me and bring some other clothes. She can help me take a shower. I'll see you at the KK when you get back."

Carlton took a quick shower, dressed in jeans and tee shirt, and jammed the cap on his head. He left her sitting in the same place at the table, phone within reach. She turned her upper body stiffly to waggle two fingers in a goodbye wave.

Luis de Silva lived in a battered twenty-foot trailer at the end of a bumpy dirt lane. Several vehicles sat up on concrete blocks beside the house. A few chickens scratched desultorily in the dirt. A porch of sorts had been created by laying tin roofing over a frame that was propped against the side of the trailer. The old man was sitting under this lean-to when Carlton drove up. He rose to his feet and raised gnarled hands in mock surrender. "Hey, policeman. Come to arrest me? I didn't do it."

Carlton laughed and teased in return. "Don't try to get away. I know everything." He shook Luis's hand and accepted a cup of luke-warm instant coffee, served in a chipped dirty cup. He asked about various relatives and heard about the latest grandchildren and great-grandchildren. One grandson was getting a divorce and moving to Los Angeles; this was the second grandson to break up his marriage. The elder sucked his teeth and reverted to Spanish in his disgust at the lack of tenacity shown by his progeny. *"Hijole!* When I married, we honored our vows. Today, they don't even go to mass."

Eventually, Carlton brought the conversation around to the murders. Had Luis heard about the killings, he asked.

"Oh, yes. My great-nephew who works at the old store there, the deli they call it now, he told me of this. And my grand-daughter, Serafina, you know her, she was there!"

"I know," Carlton said. "She found the first woman's body. Then a second one was killed, too, at my friend's house, the old *rancho*." He cleared his throat. "I found something very strange at the Bath House after the first murder. A little doll of mud, with holes poked in it. Do you know where that could have come from?"

The old man looked into his coffee cup, which wavered with the tremor of his large-knuckled hands. Carlton waited, knowing Luis would have to decide whether to trust him with family secrets. The chickens scratched and clucked. A skinny dog came around the corner and flopped at their feet. Finally, Luis spoke. "This thing you tell me is bad. Very bad. I thought no one did this anymore since my sister died. She did this, make such dolls, these *muñecas*, to hurt people. Everyone feared her, called her *bruja*." He crossed himself, and his chin sunk onto his chest. He was silent for so long, Carlton thought he had drifted into sleep. Then he spoke again, slowly, as though the words resisted saying.

"Only one knows these things today. Only one in our family wanted to learn about the dolls and the potions." He pantomimed drinking from a cup then choking. "Only one still has hate in her heart after all these years." He paused again, and his lips quivered. Carlton leaned forward to hear the next words. "Serafina. She has become a mean woman, angry with everyone. She imagines we are still the land-owners here, the *patron* family. She wasn't even born yet when we lost the land, but she listened to her Aunt Angelina and her Uncle Jesus – also to her father. They talked of it all the time."

Carlton drew back so sharply the chair legs hit the dirt with a thump, startling the dog, which rose, circled and dropped down again. "You mean – " He stopped. He must go carefully here. "The loss of the land was a terrible thing, *abuelo*. Your family has suffered, and I know Serafina has been very troubled. Can you tell me more about these dolls? Have you seen Serafina make them?"

"See her? No, no. This is secret. If a person is to be cursed, the *bruja* makes the doll at night, away from others' eyes, and hurts the doll with string." He simulated strangling. "Or with needles." He grabbed his gut and bent over as if in pain. "I cannot tell you more. I do not learn of these things. I do not wish to be a *brujo*."

Carlton knew that was all he would learn. Luis had been very generous to tell him this much, especially to name a family member. They talked a little longer – of the weather and a 1957 Ford truck parked nearby, which the octogenarian's extraordinary mechanical skills had kept running all these years. Carlton declined more coffee and took his leave.

He drove furiously down the dirt lane, his mind racing to fit this new piece of information into the puzzle. The more he thought about it, the more he was sure Serafina had made the dolls and was trying to cause mischief with them. It fit with her vindictive nature, but how did it tie into the murders? He couldn't imagine a scenario in which she was Sage's accomplice. He had searched the deck at the KK when he first arrived at the second murder scene. No doll was there, although the subsequent investigation had revealed that Serafina had been on the premises earlier that day. It would be just like her to withhold other information, too. She may have seen something else. He slammed his fist on the steering wheel. Time to have a long chat with Miss Spooky. First, however, he wanted to check on Amelie. He headed toward the KK.

CHAPTER 22

Amelie smoothed the bed and looked around Carlton's house, which was essentially a mountain cabin, fishing rod over one door, rifle over another. A neatly stacked pile of law enforcement journals sat on the floor next to a worn leather recliner in front of the woodstove. She had spent many weekends here, making love in his parents' old bed, a family heirloom with a high carved headboard. Everything in Carlton's house was worn and old but meticulously clean. She didn't have to look to know that no dust balls lurked underneath the furniture. It was a metaphor for the differences in their personalities. Her house was splashed with color in rugs, curtains, pillow covers, and paintings on the walls. Books, discarded clothing and unopened mail lay strewn about until the weekly visit from her long-time house cleaner.

Once Carlton had left, she phoned Lena, who arrived an hour later with her clothes, now washed and dried, and makeup in an overnight bag. Lena told Amelie that Ivan was still at the KK, telling her how surprised she had been that he had stayed the night. All the rooms had been available, but he had chosen the least expensive, the small room with two twin beds. She told Amelie he had been out for an early run and chortled at how good he had looked in the skimpy costume that he deemed *de rigeur* for his morning workout. Since breakfast, he and Walter had conversed continuously, and Ivan had shown an unexpected depth of knowledge about contemporary American art.

On the way to the KK, Amelie told Lena how she had rejected Carlton's offers of help. "I wouldn't have gone there last night if I hadn't been drugged. For some reason, I feel like I need this tough-girl front with him now, even though we slept together for nearly a year. If I show any vulnerability, he'll somehow infiltrate my defenses. Not in a manipulative way. God, he doesn't know how to manipulate. I just can't let him get too close."

Lena murmured assent, and Amelie absently noted an uncharacteristic lack of advice. Lena had helped her wash her hair in Carlton's shower, somehow managing to do so without getting herself soaked. Even though Lena's ministrations were gentle, the process had been painful, and Amelie felt a headache gathering at the base of her skull. They rode in silence until reaching the village, when Lena started relating some gossip about the librarian and her latest boyfriend, a Harley owner from Las Cruces who rode 300 miles each weekend to see her.

At the KK, Amelie got Walter to look over her list of artists. He reluctantly added a few names plus one more gallery he recalled that Sage had mentioned. He repeated that she should stop persecuting Sage. Then Amelie checked the Internet to see if any galleries named by Walter had web pages. She extracted phone numbers for a few of them and started dialing. She phoned galleries for dates and followed up with searches for more local newspapers. If they had no back issues on line, she called and talked to small-town editors and publishers.

Three hours later, she threw down her pencil and decided it was time for another pill. Her head throbbed, her bruises ached, and using the key-board had increased the pain in her hands and wrists. "I've got him," she announced, surprised to find that the expected feeling of triumph had been replaced with a deep sadness. Her discoveries represented horror and suffer-ing; she wished she had never heard of any of the victims. "None of the other artists Walter knows were in all those towns at the time of a murder. I found one more town where a woman was killed while Sage had a show in a local gallery, but it was ten years ago. I lucked out. The man who answered the phone had been there twenty years." She pushed herself to her feet and went to the kitchen for a glass of water, swallowed her half-pill and leaned on the counter next to Lena. "I don't see how the sheriff can ignore this evidence."

Lena looked up from kneading, shaking her head, hands locked in bread dough. "I just can't believe this. I know you didn't like Sage from the start, but I never suspected anything this horrible." Lena dropped the dough into a large bowl and covered it with a tea towel, then washed her hands. "I want to run from this. When Maria was killed, I was shocked and sad, even though I hadn't seen her in years. And I was scared for myself. Then a woman was killed here, in my place." She shuddered. "After that, the accusations diverted me into defending myself, and I let the real horror fade. But now, you're nearly killed on my doorstep, and this psycho is running loose. A man we knew! I don't know what's next." Amelie saw her dark eyes fill with tears. Amelie reached out to her friend, and they stood in the sunny kitchen, huddled under a dark cloud of confusion and terror.

Amelie sighed. "I feel like I've been keeping my feelings locked up. Then yesterday, I thought I was going to die. And now, I'm mad. I'm sick of how this has affected us all. You're scared and under suspicion of murder. Your business is down. I've been injured. Carlton is worried about his job. Walter's trust has been betrayed." She took a deep breath. "This has to stop."

Lena sighed, "I hope so. I can't get mad; I just want it all to go away." She looked through the windows to where Walter and Ivan sat companionably at the picnic table, coffee cups in hand. "Walter is going to be very disappointed," she said. "Let's see if you can convince him first. He's known Sage for years and really likes him. If he accepts that this evidence is proof enough, then you can tell the sheriff."

"Actually, I'm going to let Carlton tell the county. Maybe this will boost his reputation." If she hadn't been confined in the neck brace, she would have flung her head back to show disdain for the anxiety she felt. "Sage is a serial killer, Lena. I know I'm right about this. They're always nice and normal on the outside. Look at Ted Bundy – handsome, educated, upstanding young Republican. Killed dozens of women, probably more."

"Yeah, I think I remember his name, but it was a long time ago. Before I went to Seattle, right? How do you know about him?"

"I confess to being one of those people with a morbid fascination with serial killers. And it seemed like anyone who ever knew him wrote a book. I read a couple of them."

"And everyone thought he was a nice guy? It's hard to believe that there isn't some clue when you meet them."

Amelie got a glass from a cupboard and filled it with cold water. "I read about another one more recently in Kansas. Church leader, Cub Scout leader, married. Who would guess?"

Lena patted Amelie's hand. "Well, you had a bad feeling about Sage before I did." Lena continued to gaze at Ivan and Walter and changed the subject. "I can't imagine what those two are finding to talk about – artist and computer geek, or whatever he is. Of course, it looks like Walter goes for the weirdos, if Sage really is both artist and murderer."

"Ivan's an interesting man," Amelie said. "I don't know if he'll ever tell his story, but new aspects keep popping out and surprising me."

As if drawn by the women's attention, the two men drifted toward the house, Walter alternately talking and puffing on his pipe. Ivan bent his head to listen, hands in pockets. They slid open the door to the deck just as Carlton came in the front entrance. Amelie stifled a laugh at the look of surprise, then distaste that passed across his face at finding Ivan still there.

Carlton covered his emotions with a mask of indifference and turned to Amelie. "How do you feel?"

"Much better. I'm keeping up a steady diet of half a Robaxin every four hours and operating in only a slight fog." She fingered the stiff neck brace. "What did you find out from Luis?"

Carlton opened his mouth to answer, but Lena, the inexorable hostess, intervened. "I'll make a new pot of coffee, and we can all sit down and figure this out. Two, or in this case five, heads are better than one." Her silly cackle of a laugh let them know she was aware of the cliché.

In a few minutes they were seated in the living room. Lena, Amelie and Walter were sunk deep into the cushy sofa. Ivan sat in an arm chair, one ankle casually crossed on the opposite knee. Carlton, clearly the most ill at ease, perched on the edge of the stone bench around the fireplace, spurning Lena's offer of a cushion.

Lena, assuming the role of facilitator, nodded to Carlton. "Now you can tell us."

Carlton's eyes flicked toward Ivan. "I don't think we should talk about this now."

Lena dismissed the comment. "No, it's okay. Ivan knows everything we know – probably more. Just tell us what you learned from the old man."

Carlton turned to Amelie. "You told him," a nod toward Ivan, "about the doll?"

She attempted a shrug. "I was upset when I found it, more than I realized at first. By the time I got home, I had to tell someone."

Walter said, "Carlton, come on. Tell us if you know anything more about the dolls."

Carlton acquiesced. "Luis said Serafina was the only one he knew of who would try to put a curse on someone. Not in those exact words, but that's what he meant. I can't believe she killed anyone with her dolls, and I'm hard pressed to see how she and Sage could work together to murder anyone. I'm going to see her this afternoon and get the truth out of her if I have to – " He stopped, looked at his clenched fist and lowered his voice. "I'm going to talk to her this afternoon to see if she can help with the investigation."

Lena turned to Amelie. "Our girl here worked all morning, instead of resting, and she has some more information about Sage."

Amelie, voice still croaky, explained the results of her morning's work. "So, I don't see what other explanation there is," she concluded. "Sage was in every town at the time a woman was strangled in or near water – hot tub, river, lake. No other artist had the same schedule. Of course, I'm only check-ing on artists, but what are the odds of another person being in all these places at the same time?"

Walter sucked on his empty pipe. "I hear what you're saying, but – " He shook his head. "I just don't know. I've talked to this guy dozens of times over the years." He sank back into the sofa and sought comfort in his pipe.

Lena refilled cups, then continued to chair the meeting. "Amelie has a theory, one she shared with Carlton last night." She looked at him severely, chastising him for not bringing it up. "Go on, Amelie."

Amelie took a deep breath. "I tried applying logic to the facts because I realized I've been frustrated by trying to make the facts fit into a predetermined theory. Look, if A = B and A = C, then B must also equal C." She looked around. All faces were blank with bewilderment except Ivan's. He had the satisfied look of someone solving an especially difficult puzzle. "What I mean is, I think there are two killers. Sage undoubtedly killed the women in Bluff, Silver City, Dolores, Winslow, and Kanab." She ticked the names off on her fingers. "I believe he killed the woman here at the KK. However, he didn't kill Maria. Since we know he couldn't have been there, someone else must have done that. And," she concluded, "he couldn't have attacked me." Ivan nodded in agreement. Carlton stared at her with intense concentration.

"What's the classic question in a murder investigation, I guess in any crime investigation?" she asked.

Ivan instantly murmured an answer. "Who has motive and opportunity?"

"Right. So if we eliminate Sage as Maria's murderer, we have to look for another suspect. Who else had a reason to kill her and a way to do it?" She paused, trying not to look at Ivan because she suddenly had the feeling he had this all figured out. "Since Jenny saved my life, I think we can eliminate her as a suspect. Likewise, Rusty, despicable creature that he is, seems to have cleared himself of everything but theft."

Amelie continued. "Of all the people in the Bath House on Fourth of July, I can think of only one who knew Maria for a long time and was right there on the spot when she died." She looked expectantly at Carlton.

"Serafina? Is that who you mean? She's depressed and irrational but – "

Ivan could contain himself no longer. "This is what I want to say yesterday. Then so many events happen. I, too, analyze facts you give me and see that one person does not do these two murders. Amelie tells me of her research, old land grants, doll. This woman, Serafina, always is near killings. She has hate for Maria and Lena and all those she believe take her . . ." he groped for the English words, ". . . her ancestors' estates."

Amelie saw that Carlton bristled whenever Ivan spoke, so she was quick to co-opt his theory. "That's it. Don't you see?" She beseeched the group. Lena paced around the fireplace. Walter leaned forward to catch her failing voice. Carlton scowled at the room in general. "Serafina is obsessed with the land issues, steeped in the hatred her father, aunt and uncle had for the

Swensons from 100 years ago. From what I read, I know that Maria's grandfather and uncles were no angels; they took what they wanted by any means they could. I've no doubt they cheated the de Silva family, even if was legal in the courts at the time."

Carlton jumped to his feet. "I'm going over there right now. Serafina is sly but not very subtle. I can get her to talk to me."

Amelie struggled to be released from the sofa. "I'm coming with you this time. I know more about the land history than you do." She paused, trying not to let her voice croak. "And I'm feeling much better."

"I doubt it. Besides, this is my job. This has to be done right."

"If you were going to do it right, you'd call the county this minute. I know you don't plan to do that, so don't argue. Let's go." Amelie shoved her feet into sandals and grabbed her purse. Carlton followed her out the door.

Serafina lived in San Ysidro, about twenty minutes' drive from the Krazy Kokopelli. Carlton was silent as they sped past red cliffs and the crazy quilt pattern of old and new houses in the Pueblo. Amelie left him to his thoughts. She knew that he had to handle this on his own terms. Before he got out of the patrol car, he put a restraining hand on her arm. "I've got an idea that might rattle her cage. Just play along with me, and let's see what happens."

The adobe was cracked, and paint peeled off window frames of the little house sagging under a huge cottonwood. A dusty old Cutlass was parked directly in front of concrete steps leading to a screen door with a jagged tear in the lower corner. Dark curtains covered the windows, and the interior appeared black behind the open door. Carlton rapped sharply on the door frame, waited a few seconds and struck the door again. "Serafina! I know you're in there."

No one answered, but Amelie heard movement inside. She nearly shrieked when a cat streaked through the hole in the screen.

Suddenly, Serafina appeared, as though she had been standing next to the door the whole time. She wore her habitual long black skirt. Even on this hot day, her black blouse was buttoned tight around her neck, and long sleeves covered her arms. Looking through the rusting screen into the black background, it appeared to Amelie she was only disembodied face and hands. Inwardly, she shivered. This woman had an eerie quality; she had sensed it the first time they met on the mesa. Could she have used those pale hands to kill another human being? And – for some reason Amelie hadn't made this jump in reasoning until now – could she have attempted to strangle her yesterday? Without thinking, she put her hand to her neck brace. Serafina's eyes followed the motion, and Amelie could swear she saw an instant's look of satisfaction.

Carlton spoke. "Good afternoon, Serafina. Can we come in and talk to you?"

Serafina didn't move or respond. Her cat-like gaze observed them as though she was waiting to pounce.

Carlton repeated. "Serafina, we need to talk to you about something important."

With an abrupt movement, she pushed open the screen door, forcing them to step back as the frame swung around. "Come in," she said and waited for them to step past her into the gloom.

As Amelie's eyes adjusted to the dark, she saw a room crammed with furniture, every surface covered with scarves, dried herbs and candles. Four thick candles burned before a shrine to the Virgin of Guadalupe set on what must have once been a beautiful corner table. Melted clumps of wax stuck to the mottled surface, barely leaving room for fresh candles.

"Please sit down," Serafina motioned to a threadbare sofa covered with cat hair. "I'll make some tea."

"No tea, thank you," Carlton said. "I came with Amelie to talk to you about a deal you may be interested in. I know you don't make much at the Bath House, and Amelie here has a proposition for your land." His voice was disgustingly patronizing. Amelie started to speak, but then remembered his warning. "She's thinking of opening a gallery and gift shop. You know, tee-shirts that say 'Jemez Mountains,' cups with pictures of elk on them, paintings on saw blades, stuff like that. She wants to build a new building, made to look like an old adobe of course, and she's looking for the right land."

Serafina had started pacing as he spoke. Amelie noticed that the woman's fists were clenched. She now recognized Carlton's strategy. If he could get Serafina angry about another encroachment on the land, she might say something incriminating.

Carlton kept talking as though oblivious to Serafina's increasing agitation, describing a gift shop that would have to contain the most tasteless collection of kitsch in the world. Serafina had begun pounding one fist into the other when he delivered the coup de grace. "Amelie asked me to come along because you and I go way back. She wants to know if you'd consider selling your land with the old house on it. She really likes the location."

It was though a taut wire had snapped. Serafina shot from her chair and leaped across the room to tower over Amelie.

"Anglos! You lie, *mentiroso!*" she hissed. "Always trying to steal my land. I will stop you." Her hands rose, and Amelie saw how strong her fingers were. "You escaped once, but I will not give up and abandon my heritage." Serafina snatched at Amelie's neck brace, trying to wrench it off. Carlton shouted an order for Serafina to stop. She switched to shaking Amelie back and forth, apparently hoping to further injure her neck. Amelie pulled at the crazed woman's hands and wrists. Finding she couldn't loosen Serafina's ruthless grip, she brought one foot up and kicked, feeling her heel connect with her attacker's knee. She heard a gasp as Serafina absorbed the blow, and then the hands fell away. Amelie gritted her teeth as she sank back onto the sofa, sharp pain shooting from her neck into her back.

Carlton finally got a hold on Serafina and dragged her away from Amelie. Serafina exploded like a cyclone and whirled away from his grasp. "Don't you touch me, *pendejo*. I'll kill you, too. I'll kill anyone who tries to take our land, our *tierra*."

She retreated toward a curtain which hung in an open doorway. Carlton dropped his hands but moved slowly to his right. Amelie knew he was trying to get between the demented woman and the doorway. "Serafina," he whispered, "tell me what you did. Tell me how you avenged your family."

Serafina paused, and Amelie could see she was torn between escape and an opportunity to brag. Amelie effaced herself as much as possible, aware that Carlton and Serafina were alone in a dance of danger. They circled each other, and he never took his gaze off the feline creature whose eyes jerked now from one doorway to the other.

Serafina laughed, and Amelie knew she was hearing the sound of madness. "All my life, my father, my uncle, talk, talk, talk. How one day they would get their land back, show the Anglos. But – nothing. They talked and got drunk. Then they died."

She advanced toward Amelie but halted and tilted her head to listen when Carlton began speaking again. Amelie, ignoring the burning pain that suffused her back and neck, slowly eased from the sofa to block the front door. Serafina caught the action and swung around to watch Amelie. She crouched in preparation to leap, but Carlton sprang first. With a swift motion, he pinned her arms back and snapped on handcuffs. Amelie hadn't even seen him take them off his belt.

When the metal snapped shut on her wrists, Serafina had a fit. There was no other word for it. She jerked in a spasm, spittle flying from her mouth, and fell to the floor, sputtering and screaming incomprehensibly in Spanish. Amelie, repulsed as she was by the insanity before her, was afraid that Serafina would hurt herself. One part of her could understand the years of anger and frustration over the injustices done to the de Silva family. She stepped forward, thinking to somehow calm the manic woman. A glance at Carlton's face quelled that urge. He pulled Serafina to her feet and dragged her out to the patrol car. Amelie followed and saw Serafina writhe as the door slammed and locked.

Carlton came back to Amelie. "I have to take her to Bernalillo, and it isn't going to be pretty. Call Lena to come get you."

She nodded. "I'll walk down to the feed store."

Serafina was still struggling and screeching in Spanish as Amelie slowly walked along the highway. It wasn't far, but every muscle cried out in agony, and her medication was at the B&B. More than physical pain wracked her body. Serafina's near-confession had shaken her in a fundamental way, introducing feelings of frailty that went beyond any previous reaction to physical danger. Today, she had come face-to-face with evil. A tremor ran through her as she realized that another even more depraved monster had to be confronted and captured. She pictured Sage's handsome face. Where was he now? She wasn't given to premonition, but something made her look over her shoulder. She crossed the dirt parking lot at the feed store, taking deep breaths to quell her anxiety. This wasn't over yet.

CHAPTER 23

Amelie was sitting on a bale of straw when Lena pulled up in front of the feed store fifteen minutes later. The trembling had stopped, and a deep calm had come over her. 'Crystal-clear' had new meaning. She saw the dusty road and azure sky in brightly delineated colors. She felt each blade of the prickly straw under her thighs. Between the sounds of trucks accelerating on Hwy. 550 rose the sweet clear notes of a finch. Pungent odors from the corral behind the store filled her lungs with the joy of simply being able to breathe.

The epiphany that often came to those who escaped death had been delayed until this moment. Maybe because her pills had worn off, she told herself cynically, then mentally reprimanded herself. She was alive! She had looked into the eyes of her would-be assassin. Not alone, of course. Carlton's steely determination when Serafina's mind broke had been transmitted to her; they had stood together. She didn't know if Carlton had felt this, if he had time to even think about it, but that shared experience had created an unspoken bond that now connected them. Could that link be strengthened into a lasting relationship? A time-worn way to decide whether to take a risk was to ask, what's the worst thing that could happen? Surviving a murderous attack – twice – had to rank pretty high. Whether or not this changed things with Carlton, today was forcing her to be honest with herself about what now clearly seemed her frivolous behavior.

Lena jumped out of her truck and crushed Amelie in a hug that squeezed out a groan. She dropped her arms and stepped back. "Oh, gosh. I'm sorry. I'm hurting you. But I'm so glad to see you're okay." Riding back to the KK, Amelie couldn't seem to muster the strength to talk and gave only vague answers to Lena's frenzied questions, Amelie knew that her friend was puzzled and disappointed that she wasn't telling the story in exhaustive detail. Serene in a bubble of clarity, she did not want to diminish the feeling by dwelling on details of Serafina's revelations and tragic loss of touch with reality. In her detached state, she could feel empathy for the convoluted path Serafina had followed to become a murderer.

Lena continued to fire a stream of questions, and finally, Amelie put her hand on her shoulder and said, "I really don't want to talk about this right now. I'm as shocked as you are, and I need some time to pull back and get centered. Please, let's just don't talk."

Reluctantly, Lena assented, and they completed the drive in silence.

Amelie rolled the window down and let hot air stream into her face. She wanted to embrace the air, the insects, Lena, Carlton, all her precious friends, everything. Hold them near and leave frightening thoughts of death behind.

Once back at the KK, Lena dithered and hovered until Amelie had to ask her to stop. "Really, I'm all right. I just need to rest quietly and try to relax. Isn't this your yoga night?" When Lena reluctantly admitted that yoga started in fifteen minutes, Amelie assured her that she could get along without her for a couple of hours. Amelie hugged her as well as she could with the neck brace restricting her movements. As the truck drove away, she walked slowly to the patio, seeking respite in a familiar place. Thinking she would just rest and release the emotional overload, she leaned back to close her eyes, lulled by the river's soothing sound. She would be able to talk this through with Lena when she came back from yoga.

The sound of the sliding door roused her. Her first thought was a flashback to the day Serafina had come into the KK while Amelie was sleeping on the sofa. She knew now that Serafina had been watching for a chance to attack her, and another thought made her sit up, crying out as she strained her neck. The tea! Everything Serafina had touched was now suspect. She had to put that tea away before someone drank it. She swung her legs off the chair, expecting that Lena or Walter had returned early. A chill swept through her in a sickening wave as Sage stepped onto the patio.

His handsome visage wore a solicitous look. He came close, pressed inside her personal space and placed his hands on her shoulders. "Ah, Amelie. I heard you'd been injured. I hope you're feeling better."

Wanting nothing more than to fling his hands away and scream, Amelie quelled her trembling. "Yes, I'm much better, Sage."

He said, "I came to see Walter, but I guess he's gone. I've looked everywhere, and no one is here."

Amelie shifted back from him, feeling helpless and dominated sitting at eye level with his belt buckle. She rubbed her eyes as if she had been awakened from a deep sleep, buying time until she could think of an escape plan. Was there any way he could know she suspected him? In an attempt at trivial conversation, she said, "Sage, I thought you were on your way to Seattle. Did your plans change?"

He ignored her question and answered her unspoken thoughts. "Amelie, I came back to warn you." The tone was amiable, as if he were giving a friend helpful advice. "I'm worried that something bad is going to happen to you. Not today, not in the valley. That would be too much of a coincidence. But you are definitely hindering my activities. Some accident will have to happen on one of your little trips."

Amelie struggled to rise from the low chair, but his hands pressed her down with surprising force. Her heart was pounding, but she tried to keep her voice calm. "I don't know what you're talking about, Sage. Have you been drinking?" She strained to look up at him, but sharp pains in her neck forced her to keep her head down.

The hard hands gripped her flesh even tighter, and she gasped at the pressure on already sore muscles. "Amelie, don't mess with me. You've done quite enough harm already. Talking to all those people in my galleries. Tsk, tsk."

Even in her terror, Amelie wondered if he'd really said *tsk, tsk*.

Sage continued, "My old friend from Dolores called. Your queries reminded him that he hadn't seen any of my work for several years. Asked if I'd like to do another show." The hands had released. Now he was stroking her shoulders and upper arms. "I said I'd love to, of course. Then I talked to a few other gallery owners. Funny, they all mentioned you had called. I think I'll talk to my agent tomorrow, so I can find some new little galleries in the small towns I'm so fond of. But first, I had to see you again."

Amelie gathered her strength and surged to her feet. Her throat ached, and her voice cracked as she looked him in the eye. "Sage, you're crazy. Can't you tell you're losing control? Otherwise, you'd never take the risk to come here and confess like this."

The fake smile fell from his face, and she caught a glimpse of rage in his eyes before he replaced the mask of affability. "Confess? To what? Now I'm the one who doesn't know what you're talking about. What's risky about a simple conversation? Or are you wearing a tape recorder? Maybe I should search you to see if you're entrapping me."

Amelie stepped back as he reached for her. Behind him, she caught a slight movement at the corner of the house. Please god, she prayed silently, someone come. I don't know if he'll stay in control. In answer to that plea, Ivan stepped noiselessly into her line of sight and stood motionless, surveying the scene.

"I wish I were taping you," she answered, emboldened by reinforcements, "but it's not necessary. Lots of people know what I know. If I were gone, you'd still get arrested. That's where you're headed, you know, to prison, probably to death row." Sage was focused on her, unaware of Ivan's presence, and he was breathing harder. Amelie could not hear Ivan's footsteps over the constant hum and clatter of the river.

She took a step back and raised her voice. "You say you'll kill me, but you won't. You're too smart for that. It's too obvious."

The smirk returned to his face, and he stepped toward her again. With her back against a cottonwood tree, she could retreat no further.

Ivan chose that moment to make his entrance, calling out as though he'd just arrived.

"Hello, Amelie. I hope to find you here."

Sage moved away smoothly, and she walked on trembling legs to Ivan's side. "Yes, I came back. Do you still have a room here?"

He ignored the question. His eyes never left Sage. "You will introduce me?"

She stepped back. Whatever game this was, she'd play as long as he was on her team. "Ivan, this is Sage Hansen. He's an artist. Ivan Karnovich is a friend from Los Alamos."

Ivan extended his hand, murmuring some pleasantry, but Amelie observed the tense muscles around his mouth and in his shoulders.

Sage pretended not to notice Ivan's proffered hand. Consulting his watch, he lapsed into an affected effeminate manner. "Oh, my, look at the time. I must rush. Nice to see you, Amelie." He couldn't resist a parting shot. "I look forward to when we meet again."

He swished away in the direction of the cars, and Amelie slumped against Ivan.

"I am so glad you came. I don't think he was going to do anything here, but I'm afraid he's just about over the edge."

Ivan looked puzzled at the vernacular, and she explained. "He learned I'd been asking questions about his past. I think he's feeling the stress of knowing someone is on to him – I mean, that someone suspects him. I know he's incredibly arrogant, but I'm surprised he'd come here to taunt me."

She hugged herself, realizing that she was still trembling. Ivan put his arms around her, holding her tight against him. He soothed her and, with gentle questions, elicited her account, until she felt wrung out from the catharsis of reliving both events. When she drooped in his arms, he led her to the lounge chair. They sat thigh-to-thigh, his arm around her shoulder, while the sun sank behind the mesa and the patio dimmed in shadow.

When Carlton, Lena and Walter returned, all within minutes of each other, Ivan had left for Los Alamos, and Amelie was preparing grilled cheese and green chile sandwiches for dinner. She greeted them. "You'll never believe what just happened."

CHAPTER 24

One afternoon a month later, Amelie, Carlton, Walter and Lena were gathered around the table in Amelie's tiny dining room. Her bruises were only a memory; her psyche was another matter. Since the arrests of Serafina and Sage, she had spent many hours journaling and walking on the mesas. Those moments of looking into two killers' eyes had motivated her to look inward.

Amelie and Carlton had talked very little and only about the arrests. Today he was nearly his old self again, watchful but with an air of added confidence. Lena, holding hands with her husband under the table, looked more relaxed than Amelie could remember.

Amelie had not invited Ivan, but they had met for lunch at the Chile Works earlier in the day. Amelie knew Carlton had an important announcement about the investigation of Sage, and she didn't want the luster of his moment dimmed by the jealousy he felt for the other man. Ivan had been certain that Sage would be arrested. He said the way Sage had flirted with self-revelation when talking to Amelie indicated he was taking greater and greater risks. It was only a matter of time. In the past few weeks, Amelie had done more reading about serial killers, and she agreed that his actions that day on the patio fit a pattern of escalating behavior that often led to capture. She had also learned that having wives or steady girlfriends, which seemed beyond strange to her, was not that unusual. That answered one persistent question – his relationship with Maria.

She passed the salad, and nudged Carlton. "C'mon. Are we going to have to wait for dessert? What's the big surprise?"

Carlton swiped a napkin across his mouth. "Okay, since you can't wait. But before I tell you about Sage, I have one more footnote to the Serafina saga. Amelie, you mentioned that we should check the tea she left at the KK, and you were right on. It's valerian and betony, which would make someone very sleepy. Just like in Maria's case, sleepy enough, combined with the hot mineral bath, for Serafina to slip a thin cord around her neck and twist it like a garrote before she even knew what was happening. After she failed to get you in the river, Serafina had hoped to prepare a nice cup for you and make her job easier on the second attempt."

Amelie touched the side of her neck. The bruises were gone; she felt only an occasional twinge when she turned her head sharply. "She really was mentally ill, wasn't she? Completely delusional."

Carlton nodded. "But Sage is worse. After what seems like a million meetings, I convinced the county sheriff to contact the FBI with the information you compiled, Amelie. And surprise, surprise. They thought it was worth a follow-up. Their research found two more similar murders, going back twenty years, and they said there are probably others we'll never know about. They were able to get a warrant to search Sage's apartment in Seattle, and guess what they found?"

The others had stopped eating, faces eager with anticipation.

Lena took a sip of coffee. "Nothing too gross, I hope. I want to finish dinner."

"Not gross but strong evidence." Carlton paused for a drink of his beer. "Little trophies he'd taken from his victims, mostly pieces of lingerie, sometimes watches or earrings. Not all can be identified, but reports of missing personal items were recorded by investigators in some of the other murders. Several have matched items found in Sage's apartment, including a pair of earrings from the woman killed at the KK." Lena gasped. Walter shook his head sadly.

Amelie sighed, "He created so much misery. All those women, all those lives ruined and families destroyed."

Walter looked down at his plate, his chagrin at having defended Sage obvious. Lena reached out to take his hand. "Honey, you couldn't have known. He fooled everyone. That's why he was able to keep doing it – because he seemed like such a nice guy."

Walter shook his head and said nothing, but he continued to hold his wife's hand.

Carlton scooped salad onto his plate. "Sage was arrested by the Seattle police and is being held while they decide which murder, or murders, to charge him with – and where. It's possible he could be returned here for trial. Of course, he denies everything and has a sharp attorney, but I think his killing days are over. Thanks to Amelie."

"Here's to Miss Marple, our hero – or to be PC, heroine," Lena said, ignoring puzzled looks from the two men. They clinked their glasses.

Amelie was startled. She had never thought of herself as any kind of heroine. Her friends had needed help, and she was able to be useful to them. They would do the same for her. While they ate chicken-green chile enchiladas, she thought back over the past few months and realized there were still a few loose ends.

"What's happened to Jenny?" she asked. "Has anyone seen her around lately?"

Lena glanced at Walter and said quickly, "I heard she got fired because she got in a fight with one of the other Baca hands. I guess she left the valley because no one I know has seen her around."

"Did anyone ever figure out why she had Maria's necklace in her truck?"

Lena looked increasingly uncomfortable at the discussion of Jenny, and Carlton answered. "I understand she told the deputies that both she and Maria had identical necklaces – images of Sappho, she called them, whatever that is. When they reviewed the reports, they found that it was exactly like one found among Maria's things when she was killed. So, she told the truth. Two necklaces."

"Let's talk about something else," Lena said. "I want to forget all this as soon as possible."

"Just one more thing," said Amelie. "Where's Rusty?"

To Amelie's surprise, Lena had an answer to that. "He's gone back home to daddy in Albuquerque. He appears before Judge Garcia here next month on burglary charges. Then, he'll probably face the same charges in Sandoval County Court."

"And you know all this how?" asked Amelie.

Lena shrugged. "Well, I ran into Mary – er, Judge Garcia at the post office, and she told me about the hearing." She cleared her throat and said in a rush, "And I've been talking to his girlfriend, Ellie. In fact, I've hired her to work for me."

Carlton and Amelie said in a chorus, "You what?" Carlton added, "Walter, did you know about this?"

Walter nodded. "Let her tell it."

Lena shifted uneasily, and Amelie realized this was important to her friend, but difficult to talk about. Lena glanced at her husband, and he nodded. "She reminds me so much of myself at that age. Drifting, hooking up with the wrong people, on the brink of really messing up her life." She shrugged again. "I want to help her. Unfortunately, she isn't real bright, but I'm going to train her to do prep work in the kitchen and tend the garden."

Carlton started to protest. "But, she a thief and—"

"I know," Lena cut in. "She'll do mostly outside work for a while, all under my close supervision. If she sticks with it, I'll decide if I can trust her to clean guest rooms."

Carlton opened his mouth again, but Amelie shushed him and smiled at

Lena. "I hope it works out."

Lena gave her a grateful look and tugged on Walter's hand. "Let's go home," she said.

When the door closed behind them, Amelie went to the kitchen to clean up. She was at the sink, hands in soapy water, when Carlton came up behind and slid his arms around her waist. She could feel her breasts resting on his forearm as he nuzzled the nape of her neck.

"Leave the dishes, Amelie. Come to bed with me."

She stilled her hands, abandoning her task and thought again about the implications of having sex with him. She was afraid to disrupt the carefully wrought balance between them, to fracture the tenuous bond that had developed during the past few weeks. If she had any brains at all, she would sweetly but firmly turn him down. She had thought about this and decided she should say she needed more time alone to find her priorities. Then he thrust his hips against her and raised his hands to cup her breasts. She paused a moment longer, then stepped back from what still seemed like a dangerous precipice – a complete change in her life style. "Okay," she said, "but remember, this doesn't mean I'm making a commitment. We're just friends."